Refrain

Kennedy Ryan

Soul Series

REFRAIN is a continuation of Rhys + Kai's story from Books 1 and 2,
My Soul to Keep and *Down to My Soul*.

It should be enjoyed following those.
Thank you for reading!

Cover Art:
Emily Wittig
https://www.emilywittigdesigns.com

Editing:
Lisa Christman, Adepts Edits

Proofreading:
Kara Hildebrand

Dedicated to the readers who "demanded" more of Rhys + Kai's journey.
I'm so very glad you persuaded me to tell the rest of their story!
Thank you for being so invested and encouraging!

1

NOT TOO LONG AGO I WAS waiting tables, serving overcooked burgers and teaching dance to rambunctious teenagers. Anyone who told me then that in a year I'd be on the set of a video, performing a duet with one of hip hop's brightest stars would have gotten laughed right out of The Note. From a greasy spoon diner to the top of the music charts. It's only now that I'm accomplishing my goals that the sheer audacity of my own ambitions strikes me. Thousands of girls trek to LA, bags packed full of the same hopes and dreams I have. Only a fraction of them achieve any real success.

Even fewer find what I did. Not only am I experiencing that one-in-a-million kind of success, but I found a once-in-a-lifetime kind of love. That's the most overwhelming part of this unlikely journey.

"When's Rhyson back?" Ella, my friend and stylist, snaps the last few hooks on my skimpy leather bra top.

Every time someone mentions his name, I grin like a loon. I need to figure out not looking absolutely besotted when I hear "Rhyson."

I dip my head to spare Ella the recurring goofy grin.

"He flies back in tomorrow afternoon."

"Oh, good!" She blows at the pink strands of hair spilling onto her forehead. "He'll be back in time for your birthday."

With so much going on, I'd almost forgotten my birthday is in a couple of days.

"Yeah, he'll be home." I slip on the ridiculously high ankle boots Ella brought. "Not that we'll do much. I'm totally fine with a quiet night at home. He's been away. I just want to see him."

"Well, I'm glad he'll be back for it." Ella squats to fasten the boot buckle I can't quite reach. "It must have been something really important for him to miss Grip's first shoot."

How did I end up on the set of Grip's first shoot? No one was more surprised than I was when Grip asked me to feature on "How You Like it," his debut album's first release. It's the first thing I've done for Prodigy since Rhyson got me out of that boa constrictor contract Malcolm had me locked in. I haven't even seen Malcolm since I was in the hospital months ago. Rhyson handled everything. Well, Bristol probably handled everything. She and Rhyson orchestrated something I didn't think I'd have for years.

My freedom.

"Yeah, he wouldn't have missed it otherwise. Kilimanjaro's gonna be on After Dark, that new late show with Chip Whatshisname." I glance at my phone on the make-up table, sliding a finger over the screen to check the time. "Pretty soon on the East Coast actually."

"Is Rhyson performing?"

"Not planning to." I grimace. "Unless they corral him into it. We all know Kilimanjaro probably wouldn't be on the show this early in the game if it weren't for Rhyson as part of the package, but he insisted that they perform, not him. The segment's supposed to be about them."

Ella bends to widen one of the rips in the stretchy pants riding low on my hips, clinging to my thighs, and stopping just above the knees. With the barely-there top and the teeny, hole-y bottoms, it's a lot of skin. Thank God Rhyson is in New York and not on set. He'd have me wrapped in gingham and swaddled in cotton. I glance down past the tiny scraps of leather concealing my chest and over the rest of my scantily clad body.

"Where'd you get this outfit?" I ask with a smirk. "Hos R Us?"

"This is pretty modest compared to most videos." Ella quirks one studded eyebrow at me. "It's hip hop, honey. They want to see that booty, and you can't get away with any more clothing than this."

I glance over my shoulder at my considerable rear assets.

"These little pants make my butt look big." I fake pout at her.

"No, your butt makes your butt look big." Ella laughs at the middle finger I flash her. "At least the top makes your breasts look bigger, too. Rhyson'll like that. All guys do."

"He actually likes me just the way I am." I turn to check out my reflection and shoot a smug look at Ella when our eyes meet in the mirror. I stick out my tongue for good measure.

"I'm sure he does, Bridget Jones."

"We do that." I roll my finger in the air. "Rhyson and I, we do movie quotes."

Ella's probably tired of hearing about Rhyson, but she just gives me an "aww, that's so sweet" grin every time I mention his name. She prattles on, and I listen with half an ear, getting lost in my own thoughts. I mentally review the director's instructions for the next segment and the lyrics I need to remember and lip sync. I speed-learned the steps with the choreographer. This is my first video working with someone other than Dub. The choreographer's great, but we had to feel each other out in the short amount of time I had to prepare for Grip's shoot. The kind of artistic chemistry Dub and I had is rare, but what I have with Rhyson is rarer. I'm not second guessing my decision to cut Dub loose.

A firm knock pries me out of my musings.

"Yeah," Ella calls, hanging her black smock on the coat rack in the corner of my makeshift dressing room.

"They're ready for you, Kai," one of the production assistants says from the other side of the door.

"Okay." I glance in the mirror, taken aback by the girl staring back at me. Make up paints her face in shades of drama. Her flat-ironed hair hangs long and shiny past her shoulders. She looks like a star. I wink at her for luck. Like she needs luck. Fate must have smiled on her because all that chick's dreams are coming true.

* * *

"So how'd the shoot go?" Bristol asks from her perch at Rhyson's kitchen counter.

"Good," I mumble around a spoonful of Ben & Jerry's Half Baked ice cream. "Tomorrow we're finishing the shoot on the roof of that loft downtown."

"Great location." Bristol digs out a clump of cookie dough from her pint. "This album's gonna send Grip into the next stratosphere. And the video features two of my superstars, so of course it'll be bananas."

"Two?" I ask. "I know I signed on the dotted line with you, but I didn't think Grip had."

The first thing Bristol did once she extricated me from Malcolm's crappy contract was convince me I needed new management—namely her. With the eye roll Rhyson reserves for his twin sister, he reluctantly agreed.

"It's only a matter of time, especially now that it looks like the Qwest collaboration might actually happen. Thanks again for that hook up, by the way." Bristol flicks a hunk of dark hair over her shoulder. "I'm wearing Grip down."

"Hmmmm." I flash her an innocent smile. "And here I thought Grip was the one wearing you down."

Pink splashes over Bristol's high cheekbones. Holy crap. I'd be less shocked to see an alligator blush. Not that there's anything scaly about her. The girl's gorgeous, a softer, willowy version of Rhyson. She's just always supremely confident and assured. And unblushable.

"He won't." Bristol focuses on her ice cream. "Wear me down, I mean."

"You want him to give you a chance so badly as his manager, but you won't give him a shot?"

"Grip's not looking for 'a shot.'" Bristol presses the spoon between her full lips. "He wants a lot more than that."

I don't see the problem since I catch Bristol watching Grip all the time when she thinks no one is watching her.

"Then give it to him."

"Nah. Too risky." Bristol shakes her head and guards her eyes. "He's my brother's best friend. And we've been friends forever too. Most of all, I'm not dating someone else in the business. Those things never work out."

I tilt my head and give her a pointed look since I'm dating her brother who is very much in the business, just like me.

"Present company excepted, of course." Bristol offers an unabashed grin. "Speaking of my brother, wanna see his After Dark segment?"

For days the show has been billing the interview with Rhyson, and the segment is right on the front page of their website. As soon as the clip starts playing, I'm glad Bristol's here. That keeps me from kissing the screen, maybe even with a little tongue. I haven't seen Rhyson in more than a week. Makes me wonder how in the world I went three months without him while I was on tour. But our relationship has deepened so much even since then. We've been through so much since then. My collapse, our time alone in Glory Falls, and then all the drama with the sex tape. We've hurt each other, mistrusted each other, forgiven one another. Now there's just . . . love. Just a promise of forever we exchanged on a balmy morning in Bora Bora.

Over the last few months, I've thought about our vacation a million times. Long days and hot nights when we were the only people on the planet. Those serene waters seem like years ago instead of weeks with everything we've had going on. Launching Prodigy takes a lot of Rhyson's time and focus. I'm not sure when we'll get away again like that.

As soon as Bristol clicks the video and Rhyson comes onscreen, the ache I can only ignore for so long intensifies. His face is disciplined into the wall he fortifies and shows the public, but always drops for me. Almost from the beginning, Rhyson let me in. Inexplicably. And that's what I've missed the most this last week—the way when we're together, the rest of the world can drop away and go to Hell. It's just us, wrapped in our fiercely guarded intimacy.

"Wow," Chip, the After Dark host says, seated across from Rhyson as the band leaves the stage. "Give it up again for Kilimanjaro."

The audience applauds, and Rhyson grins, though it's a little tight around the edges. He hates this stuff. He'd better get used to it. Most label execs don't have to be this publicly involved, but they don't have their own built-in fan base or reputation as an artist the way Rhyson does. Until the listening public meets the rest of us properly through our own music, we're riding on his coattails. For now, Rhyson is Prodigy.

"They're as good as you said they were, Rhyson." Chip takes a quick sip of his water before diving in. "We heard so much about them before the performance, but of course our viewers would love to hear from you while we've got you. Gonna play for us?"

Rhyson loosens that grin just a little for the people who hoot and holler from the audience.

"This is their night." Rhyson settles deeper into the couch cushions, long denim-clad legs stretched out in front of him. "But I don't mind chatting a little. I'm an open book."

Chip smirks and shoots him a wry look because we all know Rhyson is anything but an open book.

"Well, we heard Kilimanjaro." Chip ticks off the band on one finger. "You recently signed Luke Foster, fresh off his world tour. And Grip's been everywhere for the last year, so we know what an amazing talent he is. His solo debut is on the way."

"Yeah." Rhyson pushes his long fingers through the rumpled dark hair dipping into his eyes. "Marlon's working on the first video as we speak."

"That's right. You call him Marlon," Chip says with a smile.

"Have ever since high school before there was a Grip." Rhyson grins and shrugs. "He'll always be Marlon to me."

"And a little birdie told me that Kai Pearson features on his first single. We got glimpses of Kai on Luke's tour, but we're all excited to hear more from her. She just signed to Prodigy too, right?"

If the wall was up before, it's reinforced with steel after Chip's question, but the small smile playing on Rhyson's lips never budges. If the eyes are the window to the soul, Rhyson draws frosted shutters over his better than anyone I know.

"Yeah. Kai's with Prodigy now." He lowers his lashes, tracing an invisible pattern on his knee. "We're lucky to have her."

"Obviously, you know talent," Chip says. "A lot of people wonder how Kai has risen so quickly. Out of nowhere, in Luke's video. Then opening for him on tour. Now featured on the debut single of arguably the most anticipated hip hop album this year. What would you say is so special about her?"

Rhyson quirks his grin to the left and links his hands across his stomach, looking back up at Chip.

"Where do I start?" A full-blown smile sprouts on his face. "Kai has more raw talent than probably anyone I've ever met. When you pair that with her work ethic and such diverse gifts, singing and dancing . . . and acting eventually . . . she's just a once-in-a-lifetime kind of artist."

"You wouldn't be biased, would you?" Chip teases. "It's no secret that you and Kai are in a relationship. Is that the boyfriend or the label exec talking?"

Rhyson's smile dissolves.

"I don't do bias." Annoyance narrows his eyes. "It's definitely no secret that Kai and I are together since people won't leave us alone for some reason, but anyone who knows me understands how important music is to me. I wouldn't offer the public something that wasn't legit. And Kai is legitimately that talented. I think because she's also gorgeous, people sometimes want to believe that her looks or who she's dating got her where she is so fast. I wouldn't say it's been fast since she's been working toward it all her life. The only person tougher on Kai than me is Kai herself. Believe me. She's the real deal. No one can take that from her."

I absorb his affirming words like rain. My wide eyes find Bristol's. We share a grin before returning our attention to the screen.

"Well said." Chip chuckles. "Since you brought it up, where do things stand with you two? Very public breakup last year. Quietly reunited. Now there are rumors you're living together. Here's your chance to clear everything up."

"If there was anything I needed to clear up," Rhyson says with a quick grin and a hard look, "You think I'd wait till I'm sitting on your couch to speak about my private relationship?"

Chip's smile falters a little before firming back up.

"I'm just saying people are fascinated by the two of you. Tell us what's next for you guys."

"Prodigy has a showcase in Vegas in a few weeks, so you'll get to see all of the artists, including Kai, then. After the showcase, we'll start focusing on her solo debut."

"You've told us a lot about what's next professionally," Chip says, a determined set to his mouth. "But what about personally? What's next for you and Kai as a couple? Is it too soon to hear wedding bells?"

"We're thinking about songs, not bells right now." Rhyson's smile relaxes the line of his mouth. "We're very much focused on now, not on what's next."

That's the right answer. I know that. The impromptu vows, the promises we exchanged in Bora Bora were just for us two. Rhyson's incredibly private. We both are. We'll know when the time is right to take those next steps for everyone to see. And it's enough, right?

I marry you. I marry you. I marry you.

The pledge we shared is never far from my heart. Somehow hearing him say we're focused on now and not considering what's next feels like a pebble in my shoe. A tiny thing, but bothersome and causing a little discomfort. We haven't talked about a wedding or marriage again. There's been so much going on. I didn't even realize until right now, in this moment, how much I've wanted us to at least talk about it. It's ridiculous, but there it is. I don't want Rhyson to feel trapped by what we said that day. Not that he would, but I can at least be honest with myself and say that I want to marry him. Officially. For-the-world-to-see marry him.

"Thanks for being with us," Chip concludes, extending his hand to Rhyson. "And thanks for bringing Kilimanjaro by. I know that's not the last we'll see of them."

Rhyson shakes his hand, but looks directly into the camera and tugs on one ear. My heart somersaults in my chest. That will never get old. Just that little gesture always tells me that even when he's in front of millions, his mind's on me.

"Guess that was for you, huh?" Bristol stands to open the cabinet under the sink hiding the trash so she can dispose of her empty carton. "I've seen him do it enough now to know."

Heat inches up my neck and over my cheeks. I just nod.

"It's kind of our thing." I toss my empty pint, missing the trash can by a few inches. Bristol picks it up for me and finishes the job. "Thanks. My aim isn't great."

"Oh, I think your aim is just fine. You get what you set your sights on." Bristol leans a hip against the marbled counter. "And that wasn't a subtle dig about you using my brother to get ahead."

"Good." I tilt my neck to both sides, trying to alleviate some of the tension resting on my shoulders. "Then what did you mean?"

"You're ambitious, but like Rhyson said, you back it up with talent and work ethic."

This may be the first real compliment Bristol has ever paid me. I give her a cautious glance like she's a Trojan horse.

"Um . . . thanks?"

"I do have a point here." Bristol laughs and leans forward an inch, narrowing her grey eyes in speculation. "Rhyson mentioned acting, and I know when you first signed with me, we talked about it some. Do you seriously want to pursue it?"

"Eventually." I twist my lips to the left. "With the right timing and the right part."

"What if I told you I might have the right part and the time may be now?"

"A part?" I touch my chest. "For me?"

"I emailed you the script yesterday." Bristol grabs her phone, tapping and scrolling until she finds what she's looking for. "Yep. Sent it last night. You didn't get it?"

"I haven't checked my email in forever." I sigh and lift the hair off my neck. "Gep insisted I get a new cell since my old number was floating all over town on job applications and audition call sheets. I haven't set up email on the new one. Half my contacts didn't come over, and my calendar is somehow screwed up since none of my appointments have been showing. I hate changing phones."

"Well, check your email when you get the chance because I sent some other documents over I need you to read through." She reaches down into her bag. "Fortunately for you, I'm not so modern I don't mind killing a few trees."

She plops a thick bound script onto the counter.

"Some light reading for you." She watches me closely. "The director specifically asked for you. It's a supporting role, a dancer. The part is made for you really. I think it's yours for the taking, but they want you to come in for an audition."

This is a lot to process. For years my life felt like this little red wagon dragging behind me, slowed down by every crack in the sidewalk and getting hung up on every clump of grass. Now my life is the autobahn—a super highway where I'm on tour one day, in music videos the next, and auditioning for movies without time to even change lanes.

Before I can respond, Rhyson's ringtone, his song "Lost," hums into the quiet kitchen. Bristol glances at the screen, smiling when she sees her brother's handsome face.

"I'll let you get that. Tell him I said hi and great job tonight." Bristol grabs the bag holding her laptop and God knows what else, gesturing to the mammoth script on the counter. "Read that and thank me later."

She's left the kitchen by the time Rhyson's deep voice wraps around my nerve endings. I forget about the script, about Bristol, about my early call time for tomorrow's shoot.

"Pep."

Just that one word. The name only he calls me. My fingers stray to the nameplate necklace resting warm and solid on my chest just below my grandmother's gold chain.

"Rhys, hey." A knot swells in my throat. "I miss you."

"That's my line. I bet I miss you more." He chuckles, but sounds tired. "Did you see the show tonight? The guys were great."

"Yeah." I hop up onto the counter, swinging my legs to kick my feet against the base. "They were amazing. So were you. You even kept your cool when Chip asked about us."

"Barely." Rhyson pushes his irritation out in a puff of air. "Why can't people leave us the hell alone and stay out of our business?"

"You shouldn't be so fascinating." I laugh and pull up one knee, resting my heel on the counter so I can examine my foot, slightly puffy and pink from the long day dancing in six-inch heels.

"Me?" His husky laugh skitters across my skin, and I imagine his breath on my neck. "Everyone left me alone until you showed up."

We both know he was walking around disguised in moustaches long before me.

A burst of noise in the background intrudes from his end.

"What's that?" I ask. "Where are you?"

"Some club. Hold on a sec."

Some club? I assumed he was safely tucked in for the night in his New York apartment at . . . I flip my phone around to check the time . . . one o'clock in the morning on the East Coast.

"This is the guys' first time in New York," Rhyson says. "They wanted to go out after the show. I'm back behind the club. The only quiet spot I could find."

"Behind the club?" Now I'm nervous for a completely different reason. "Are you alone in some alley, Rhyson? Is that safe? Be careful."

"Damn, Kai. I'm a little insulted. I can take care of myself, you know."

"I know." I still have to ask. "Where's Gep?"

"Just inside the club. Not even a hundred feet away. I thought you might want me all to yourself for some quick phone sex?" There's hope in his voice.

"In your dreams, buddy. You're out at some club at one o'clock in the morning, and I'm holed up here at your house on the other side of the country. No phone sex for you."

"Believe me. I'd rather be there with you." Rhyson pauses before saying softly. "And it's our house, not just mine."

I don't even try to fight the smile that floats up from my feet over every inch of me until it reaches my face.

"How'd the shoot go today?" he asks.

"Exhausting, but good." I roll my head, stretching to reach the knotted muscles in my neck.

"How, um . . . was the choreographer?"

Not as good as Dub.

Cypher, Grip's director, offered to use Dub since he knew we'd worked so well together in the past. Of course, that wasn't an option. Rhyson would've flipped, so I left the choreographer to the director's discretion.

"The choreographer's fine." I keep my voice even and hope he won't pick at this scab.

"But you prefer Dub." He says it, not asking the question.

"I prefer not arguing with you." I blow some of my weariness from the day out in a long sigh. "If you're asking if the choreographer is as good as Dub, then no, she's not."

"Ask me to compromise on something else, Kai." Rhyson's words come out terse. "But not this."

"I haven't asked you to compromise on this, and I won't."

I don't let myself think about how good Dub and I were together. It's a rare chemistry we have as dancer and choreographer. We'd even already brainstormed my first video incorporating a series of tunnels downtown for the routine. It wouldn't be right for me to use it with someone else. It's just as much his creation as mine. Probably more.

"If he could keep it professional, we wouldn't be dealing with this," Rhyson says. "But I know he can't do that."

"I agree."

"You do?" The question comes with caution.

"I do. Dub showed his hand pretty clearly right before the last show. His interest went beyond professional, and I don't want that anywhere near our relationship."

"What does that mean?" Rhyson's words plow across the line. "Showed his hand how?"

"It doesn't matter now." I chew on my lip, wishing I hadn't even mentioned it because Rhyson will—

"Pep, showed his hand how?"

Persist.

"He just made a few comments before the last show that confirmed you were right about what he . . . um, wanted."

"Wanted? From you? What did he say?"

"Just that—"

"All of it, Pep," he demands.

"I don't remember word for word, Rhys."

"Okay, gimme the words you do remember."

"This is irrelevant. You know I'm not working with him."

"Exactly. So tell me what the hell he said." Rhyson pauses before adding in a more civilized tone, "Please."

"He just said that if you weren't in the picture, he'd already be in my bed."

"Even if we weren't together, he wouldn't have a shot. Not with no dick because I'd cut it off before I'd let him anywhere near you."

So much for civilized.

"Castration seems a bit extreme." I know he hears my grin because he finally laughs, the air loosening between us just a little.

"I'm sorry," Rhyson finally says, his voice freed of the growl. "I just know he's wanted you from the beginning, and even talking about him irritates the hell out of me."

"Rhys, they're ready," Gep's deep voice and the muted noise from inside the club reach me. My heart goes leaden. I know what's next, and I'm not ready for it.

"I gotta go, babe." Rhyson huffs a frustrated breath. "I'm not doing a great job babysitting these guys. They wanna check out this, um . . . other club tonight. It's all they've been talking about."

"Another club?" I know him too well not to detect the discomfort in his voice. "Which club?"

The silence between us grows viscous with his discomfort and my suspicion.

"It's a club called Pirouette."

Even I've heard of the exclusive ballet-themed, members-only strip club.

"I see." I lay a slab of stone to cover the hurt in my voice and fake a yawn. "Well, I'm really tired and have this early call time for the last day of shooting tomorrow. So I—"

"I'm not staying," he says quickly. "It's a by-invitation-only kind of place, and I know the owner. He's actually a good friend of mine."

I hop off the counter, turn off the overhead lights and start up the rear kitchen staircase, dragging that ball of lead where my heart should be, getting heavier by the second, with me.

"You don't have to explain." I press my fingers to my temple, the thought of my Rhyson in some strip club with naked women willing to do just about anything for a night with him drives a stake through my head.

"I want to explain." His next words are lower and not directed at me as if he's turned his head. "I'm coming. Just gimme a damn minute. Pep, you still there?"

"Yep." I pop the "p," keeping my response as short as the rein I have on my temper. "I don't want to hold you, though. They're obviously . . . eager."

"I'm not going there for me."

"Oh, you sacrificial lamb," I bite out, drizzling the words with sarcasm. "Poor Rhyson, held hostage in the strip club."

"Kai, I promise you I'm getting the guys in and then going back to the apartment and jerking off to a picture of you in that black bikini."

"I don't care if you . . ." I process what he said, his words settling like tiny snowflakes and cooling my anger as they gradually sink in. "You're what?"

"I've already jerked off three times today," Rhyson says abruptly, drawing a labored breath from the other side of the country. "This morning in the shower. After lunch in the bathroom stall, and right before tonight's show in the dressing room. My balls haven't been this blue since I was fourteen, and it's not because of some random tits in a fucking strip club. It's because I haven't been inside of you in over a week."

"Rhyson, I—"

"So you can be angry that I'm dropping the guys off at Pirouette," he continues. "Be irritated over nothing if you want. As long as you know that when I get home, wherever I find you is where I'm fucking you."

And just like that, the besotted grin I still haven't figured out how to squelch spreads over my face again.

"Sarita washed our sheets yesterday," I whisper, stopping in the hall leading to our bedroom and sliding down the wall to sit on the floor. "I almost cried because the new ones didn't smell like you."

"You think that's bad," Rhyson says, a grin embedded in his fatigue-roughened voice. "I brought a pair of your panties with me to New York."

"The red ones I left on the bathroom floor?" I laugh and stretch my legs out in front of me. "I spent ten minutes looking for those because I just knew I didn't put them in the hamper. I didn't know I had a stalker."

"You can't stalk what's yours." His voice dips and darkens, towing the conversation into deeper waters. "You're mine, right?"

His words shorten my breath and tighten my nipples and wet the panties I'm wearing right now.

"You know I am." It slips past my lips, a constricted wisp of words.

"I swear to you I'm not staying at Pirouette, babe," he says softly, reminding me of the tension that has melted in the warmth of the last few moments. "I'm just getting the guys in and then going home."

"Guys go to strip clubs all the time. It's no big deal."

It's amazing how I find the inner rational and understanding girlfriend now that I know he's leaving the guys at the club.

"I used to go there a lot," he admits. "I haven't been back since we met. I don't need to see anyone else. Just you. There isn't room for anything else, Pep. I can barely focus in these meetings thinking about you. Missing you."

I close my eyes, my hips shifting with the memory of him between my legs, slamming into me, eyes imprisoning mine above me.

"I miss you so bad, Rhyson." I press my lips against my teeth, trapping a needy moan inside my mouth. "It feels like it's been months instead of a week. I can't wait for tomorrow."

"Yeah, about that." Something about his sigh on the other end splashes icy water all over my heated body. "I probably won't be home tomorrow, but I promise I'll be back in time for your birthday."

I stifle a groan. That bed upstairs is so cold and lonely with him gone, but I've slept alone most of my life. I can last without him. I know that rationally, but it doesn't mean I won't wake up tomorrow clutching his pillow and sniffing our sheets for some trace of him like a lovesick hound.

"That's okay," I lie. "Another meeting?"

"Um, yeah. Unavoidable."

I try not to whine, but every part of me aches for him. My body churns with need. My heart strains behind my breastbone like it's seeking him.

"What is it?" I ask, even though it doesn't matter. All that matters is that I have to get through an extra day, sleep through another night alone.

"I have something to take care of." His voice tucks something away. Is it guilt? Why is he being evasive? "I really have to go if these guys are gonna get in tonight."

"Okay." I try to ignore the niggling thought that he's keeping something from me. "I guess I'll see you in two days."

"Yeah and don't forget what I said. Wherever I find you—"

"You're fucking me." I laugh even as my eyelids start drooping under the weight of all today entailed.

"That's my girl."

2

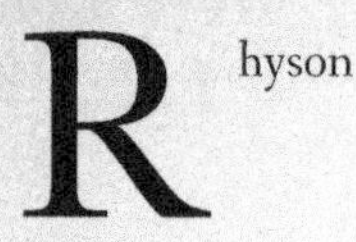hyson

HOME.

It's a concept that has evolved over the years. Growing up, home was a sprawling New York estate that somehow managed to make me feel claustrophobic every moment I was there and not on the road performing. Later home became my uncle Grady's modest Los Angeles cottage, where I was surrounded by music and students, and most of all, unconditional love for the first time. For the last few years, home's been my Calabasas mansion, gated and exclusive, hiding me from the prying eyes of the world. But now and for the rest of my life, Kai is the living, breathing address that is my home. She's my entire damn zip code.

In the back seat of Gep's SUV, I check my impatience with the unreasonable traffic on the way home from the airport.

"It's fucking midnight." I find Gep's eyes in the rearview mirror. "What's the hold up?"

"It's LA, Rhys," Gep says through barely-moving lips. "We're almost there."

I bounce my knee and flick a disparaging glance at the wild flowers wrapped in tissue paper on the back seat beside me.

"These flowers are stupid, aren't they?" I ask. "She probably won't even like them. I should have found some mistletoe. Why'd you let me buy these lame flowers at the airport?"

"Since when do I 'let' you do anything?" Gep's laugh rumbles in the subdued luxury of the car. "And Kai won't hate them. She's a girl. Girls like flowers."

"Kai's not girls, and she was pretty irritated with me last night."

"Well, you go to a strip club, tell her you're coming home a day late and don't tell her why." Gep's mountainous shoulders lift and fall. "Go figure."

"It'll work out." I smile just a little despite the traffic slowing us down. "She'll see tomorrow. The flowers are for tonight."

Because tonight, I'm sleeping with my girl. Exhaustion tugs my shoulders down. The motion of the car practically lulls me to sleep. No world tour, however grueling, could prepare me for the nonstop demand of building a record label from the ground up. But I don't care how tired I am, before I give in to sleep I'll satisfy this itch, this agitation that's been burning just beneath my skin for days. Yes, to be inside of Kai, but it's deeper than that. It means more than that. She has become my constant urge, and being away from her this long makes me physically ache.

I absently massage the small, but persistent pain in my right hand. The experts keep telling me it should be fine and pain-free, and that I won't be able to tell the difference once I start playing again. Only it hasn't stopped hurting and I haven't played. Not in public at least. Even when I play alone, I'm afraid it sounds . . . different than before. If I hear it, won't everyone else?

"We're here." Gep twists from the front seat to scan my face in the light from my driveway floodlights.

I drag both hands over my face and nod, grabbing the wild flowers that seemed perfect at the airport but now seem silly. At the rear of the SUV, I pull my bag out and wave off Gep's offer to take it inside.

"I'm good." I offer a weary salute and a wearier smile. "See you tomorrow."

"Morning?" Gep's eyebrows scoot up his forehead to the edge of his buzz cut.

"Nah." I start toward the house, flipping my suitcase to its wheels and dragging it behind me. "We'll sleep in. I have one appointment, but I'd prefer to handle that alone."

"You sure?"

"Yeah. I'll be fine in the morning. Tomorrow night, you and the rest of the team should be enough. I think you already have the details."

"Good enough." He climbs back in and gives me one final nod. "She'll love the flowers."

I roll my eyes and haul the bag inside, the sound of the SUV pulling off the last I hear of Gep. The house is completely still like an undrawn breath, the wide foyer floor spotless. The faint scent of the cleaner Sarita uses lingers in the air. I'm too tired to drag my heavy bag up the staircase so I leave it at the bottom step. I'll get it before Sarita arrives and takes it upon herself to move it, but right now, I just can't.

The first thing I notice when I enter our room is the lingerie laid out on the bed. One of the vibrantly colored sets I brought home for Kai a few weeks ago. Alternatives to her footed Jackson Five pajamas. She's never worn the flimsy piece, but my dick stiffens behind my zipper as I imagine Kai's tight, curvy body caged in the decadent cups and strips of silk.

"Kai?"

I glance around the empty room, knowing I'm not overlooking

her, but needing to call her name. I step into the spacious closet, the sight of her things still populating one half of it diffusing my mild and irrational panic. I'm just about to head downstairs and check the music room when the smell of pear and cinnamon invades the air around me, wafting from the bathroom.

I lean against the bathroom doorjamb and savor the sight of Kai stretched out in the bathtub, candles lit around its edge. Most of the bubbles have dissolved, and her nipples peekaboo through the skimpy suds. A thick, bound manuscript of some sort is propped on her stomach, submerged in the water. Her head rests on a bath pillow behind her, and her small feet don't even reach the other end of the tub but disappear under a delicate mound of leftover bubbles.

I just take her in. After more than a week apart, this first moment all I want to do is look at her. Reassure myself that she's real. That we've weathered all the storms so far, mostly of our own making, and she really does live here with me. She really does sleep in my bed. She really is mine.

Wet hair slicks back from her face, exposing the curve of her cheekbones and the dark slash of her thick eyebrows. Her chest lifts almost imperceptibly with slumbered breaths.

My practical mind tells me that I'm as tired as she probably is after Marlon's shoot. I should just scoop her up, dress her in one of her vintage nightshirts, cuddle, and call it a night. My heart softens at the picture of exhaustion she makes. But my mind and my heart aren't the only ones with a vote. It's a decision by committee, and apparently my dick is the chairman of the board because I'm toeing off my shoes, dropping my jeans and peeling my t-shirt over my head before I can guilt myself out of having what I've been craving for days.

I told her I'd fuck her where I found her. I'm nothing if not a man of my word. I flick the lever to drain the water. The sound causes Kai's eyelids to flutter, the arc of sooty lashes casting shadows under her eyes.

"Rhys?" Her eyes widen a little before a smile blossoms on her face.

"Hey, honey." I pull down my boxers and free my erection. "I'm home."

She glances between my face and my dick like she's not sure which she should kiss first. Her breath quickens. The slow drag of her tongue across her lips mesmerizes me. I step into the tub, naked and hard.

"What are you doing?" She sits up, plucking the soggy script from the water and dropping it to the bath rug.

"What does it look like I'm doing? I told you I was fucking you where I found you."

"Rhyson, not in here. I actually have lingerie this time." Kai puts her elbow on the tub, leveraging herself to stand. "Let me—"

"Nope. This is where I found you."

I lift her so I can slide into the space she occupied, and then settle her over my legs. Her thighs slide across me, wet and firm and slick, as she adjusts herself more comfortably.

"Just let me look at you for a minute, Pep."

She stops squirming, going still above me, resting her forearms against my chest and shaping her hands to either side of my neck, her thumbs wandering over my eyebrows and lips. I press a hand between her shoulder blades until her breasts rest against me and her heart trebles into my chest. Our eyes lock, and for the first time, the agitation eases. That burning urge that's had me jerking off three times a day quiets even though we're still not fucking. Of course, I've missed making love to my girl, but this is what I really needed. The mere physical wasn't what my body, my heart was calling out for. It was this. The closeness of her breath misting my lips. Of her forehead resting against mine. I haven't pierced her flesh, but I'm already inside of her in the way that truly counts, already occupying her soul. There is no greater intimacy than this moment we've wrapped each other inside of, unable, unwilling to look away. I barely breathe I'm so afraid I'll shatter this rare, fragile bubble we've blown for ourselves.

In so many ways, beyond these walls, I have the world at my feet, but the sum of my desires is in this bathtub. Naked and content and just the two of us.

"Let's not ever lose this, okay?" she whispers, rubbing our noses together and brushing her lips across mine. "Promise me."

"I'm going to spend the rest of my life loving you." I reach up to caress the fullness of her mouth, stained red from the heat and steam of her bath. "That's a promise."

Something flicks across her face. Uncertainty? A question?

"What is it?" I lift her chin to study her face straight on, to see if I can catch that expression again. Get to the bottom of it.

"Nothing." She glances down at the space between our bodies and then up at me, a bit of humor bending her lips into a smile. "You just promised to fuck me where you found me, and so far, you're not doing a very good job of it."

I push the heavy wet hair back so I can see the golden skin of her shoulders and breasts. My hands curve at her hips, lifting her until her nipples hover at my mouth.

"Where do you want me to start?" I breathe the words over the tight, raspberry tips of her breasts.

Her throat works in a convulsive swallow before the words tumble past her lips in a heavy rasp.

"My breasts." She closes her eyes. "Please, Rhys."

"Look at me." I wait until her eyes open and fix on me again. "I will, but you have to watch."

My eyes sear into hers as I pull one nipple into my mouth. Damn, it's good. I pull it deeper, capturing as much of her breast as my mouth can hold. I'm not gentle. She doesn't want me to be. Hearing the rough suction of my lips around her only makes me harder. I could come from this. Just from suckling her breasts and from the motion of her hips moving restlessly against me and seeking the same relief in me that I seek in her. She's spread over me, her wet thighs splayed across mine, but I still haven't entered her. Her eyes never leave my lips latched around first one breast and then the other, arousal lengthening her nipples. Her mouth falls open, a moan wrenching from her throat, and her fingers dissolve into my hair.

"Oh, God, Rhyson. I'm so ready. Right now. Please."

I ignore her pleas, leaning into her so my lips brush the pillowed flesh of her earlobe.

"Now where do you want my fingers, Pep?"

She shudders against me, rising up as if she plans to connect us, like she'll take it if I won't give it to her. I push her gently back.

"Not yet, baby. Tell me where I should put my fingers."

"Touch me." She briefly squeezes her eyes shut before looking back to me, passion swallowing the irises into a dark pool. "Just touch me."

"Where?" My hands tremble with the promise of bathing my fingers in her body's juices. "Where should I touch you?"

She swallows again, lowering her lashes before looking back to me, desire boldly shining from her eyes.

"My pussy. I want your fingers in my pussy."

"Fuck yes," I choke out, slipping two fingers between the thick, slick lips, sliding them up and down until she's dripping for me. My thumb searches out her clit, wet with longing, while my two fingers thrust relentlessly inside of her. "Like that?"

She nods jerkily, her breath stuttering. My fingers fuck her until they're lost in the slippery flesh. Her hips become frantic over my hand.

"Can you take another?" I don't wait for her response before pushing a third finger inside.

"Ahh, yes." Her back concaves, breasts thrusting into my chest. I bend to recapture a nipple, suckling and biting until I know she'll wear my marks the next day, but she doesn't complain. She pleads for more. For me to never stop. She reaches between us, wrapping her small hand around my cock, tugging gently, rubbing her thumb over the head until it's damp and swollen.

"Is this mine, Rhyson?"

I jerk in her hands, heat crawling up my legs and seething in my balls. I don't know what arouses me more. The sure, firm motion of her hand, or the possession of her words. The way her eyes claim me.

"You know it is, Pep. Every inch is yours." I don't just mean every inch of my cock. I mean every inch of my body. Every acre of my heart. Every ounce of my soul, poured out like an offering for her to do with as she pleases.

"If it's mine, then I can have it whenever I want, right?" She tightens her thighs around mine, suspends herself over me. "Am I right, Rhys?"

"Whenever you want, Pep." I groan into the satiny scented skin of her neck, biting gently. "Dammit, take it now."

And she does. She slides onto me, a scalding clasp of flesh. That first thrust steals our breath at the same time, pounds our hearts together, twines our souls into one accord. Rising, falling, she milks me with tight, shallow pumps, her movements barely perceptible, but rippling through me. She captivates me with the tiniest undulation of her hips and takes me so deep I'm sure I'll come out on the other side of her.

Her nails claw into my scalp, stirring a sharp pain into the bliss. She digs her fingers into my shoulders, gripping to hold on as I thrust into this tight, slick fantasy. I piston up and into her with enough force to break her, but she clutches me. Clings to me.

I don't want to come. I want to fuck her infinitely. If I could seal us in this moment, preserve it in amber, I would. I'm not just inside her body. We inhabit each other's souls. And this thing watering her eyes, clogging my throat, clamping my chest, it's more than emotion, more than a feeling that could fail or flee. It's the most precious thing I've ever had. If this is light, it's blinding until she is all I see. If this is sound, it's music. We are the verse, we are the chorus. And as we come together, her cries harmonizing with mine, this love resounds. It's loud; so deafeningly loud that all I hear is her. And all she hears is me. We are our own refrain.

3

ai

I WAKE WHEN IT'S NOT YET day. Not quite dawn. Today is my birthday. I was born at 5:10 a.m. I wonder if the sky outside Glory Falls Memorial Hospital looked like this to my mother. Painted with promise and not yet bright with morning. Maybe that's the reason dawn was her favorite time of day. Maybe I was the reason.

Grief is just as much about holding on as it is about letting go. I haven't felt that gut-deep hurt when I think of Mama in weeks. Perversely, I miss it. That pain keeping her memory so close to the surface of my life made forgetting her, forgetting even one moment we had together, impossible. Some days I feel guilty about the happiness I've found. Here with Rhyson. In my career. In my life, but then I realize it's all she ever wanted for me. To live my dreams with a man who loved me deeply and truly. Something she ultimately didn't have.

We never closed the drapes last night. There's now just enough light intruding through the window for me to see the aggressive angles and the elegant masculinity of Rhyson's profile. He's sprawled beside me, his dark hair messy on the pillow and spilling into his eyes. The sheet has slipped low, baring the strong arms and shoulders, inked in a vivid mosaic of musical notes and lyrics. I can see the firm, muscled curve of his ass. Red faintly stripes the tanned skin where my nails scored him, urging him deeper into my body. The memory of riding him last night whirs a storm cloud in my core. Last night and the promise of more this morning.

If he ever wakes up.

Geesh, he's the one who's been living on East coast time for the last week. You'd think he'd be up well before me, but his body's clock seems to be adjusting just fine to this coast, and he's fast asleep. And I've been awake for what feels like ages.

It's not excitement about my birthday that has me awake so early. Something keeps bothering me. Like I've forgotten something. Neglected something. Left something undone. I've felt that way for days, but if my subconscious knows what it is, it's not revealing it to me.

With a small sigh, I turn my attention back to the iPad in my lap. I haven't picked it up in weeks. Before I fell asleep in the bath, I was reading the script Bristol left. Now that it's a soggy, ruined mess, I opened her email to continue reading the soft copy she sent. The script's good. Really good. I'm not sure I'm good enough to play the supporting role the director has in mind for me. Sure, I took theater in high school and starred in a few school plays, but is that enough to prepare me? I haven't even started acting classes yet.

My inbox was overflowing with unopened emails. I'll go through them all later, but Bristol's were right on top. I'm refocusing on the script when a warm hand, tipped with a musician's calluses, strokes my thigh under the sheet. I fight the shiver my body involuntarily surrenders, keeping my eyes focused on the tablet. When his fingers slip over my knee, tugging until my legs stretch open, I still don't acknowledge him. I don't react when his head disappears under the sheet. It's only when I feel the first long swipe of his tongue that I . . .

"Holy crap," I whisper, tossing the tablet to the thick rug so I can grip the headboard with one hand and slide the other under the covers to fist his silky hair. His head bobs under the sheet with a thorough exploration, biting my lips, licking in the crevices, sucking my clit until I'm saturated. I'm so close. Oh, God, I'm gonna come.

But then he stops.

He pokes his head out from under the sheet, lips shiny and wet, a wide, devilish grin hanging between his lean cheeks.

"That'll teach you to ignore me." He laughs at the evil eye I give him and slides up my body until he's right above me, carrying my scent on his lips.

"Happy Birthday, baby." He drops a kiss on my mouth before scooting up and propping his shoulders against our tufted headboard. Even in my unfulfilled state I can't help but smile at him. He's home.

"Thank you for making it home in time." I gesture to the wildflowers in the vase by the bed. "And for those. They're beautiful."

"I never pegged you as a flowers kind of girl." He gives me a searching look like he's trying to figure out if I'm lying about liking them.

"Never have been." I lean over to smell the flowers. "But I love anything you give me."

His eyes go softer before he leans in and whispers across my lips.

"You keep making me fall in love with you over and over and over. When does it stop?"

"It won't stop."

I drop my head to his shoulder and run my hand over his chest and down the muscled rung of abs. He pulls my head deeper into his neck, sniffing my hair and leaving a kiss on top.

"I missed waking up with you," I confess, like he didn't already know.

"You did?" The morning huskiness of his voice is so sexy. That's the first thing I missed.

"When you wake up, you're relaxed and open in a way I don't see at any other time of the day."

"Too much crap to do as soon as I'm out of bed," he mutters, scraping a hand over his sleep-mussed hair.

"Yeah, but I get to see it. I get to see you that way, and I think I'm the only one."

"That's because I save the best parts of myself for you. The mornings are for you." He angles his head until he's poised over my lips. "And you get them for the rest of our lives."

He takes my lips in a slow claiming, sliding his fingers into my hair and licking deeply into my mouth. He moans, or maybe it's me. Maybe it's a sound we make together. I slow the kiss until it's just a breath between our lips because I want to tell him something before I forget.

"Rhys, speaking of the rest of our lives." I pull back just enough to study his face. "When Chip interviewed you, he asked if you heard wedding bells."

Something flares in his eyes, but it comes and goes so quickly I don't have time to process it. I force myself to say what I've been thinking since the After Dark interview.

"I know we said a lot of things in Bora Bora."

"Which things do you mean, Pep?" The corners of his eyes crinkle with his grin. "Because we did say a lot of things. Like that one time you said, 'Oh, God. Right there, Rhyson. That's it. Yes! Oh, God, yes!'"

A blush scalds my cheeks.

"And I do recall you saying, 'Don't you stop. Don't you dare stop, Rhyson. I'm so close.'" He looks at me with false innocence. "You mean those things?"

"I love you," I grit out, fighting back my grin. "But I can't stand you."

Laughter shakes his shoulder against me. I punch him lightly before soldiering on.

"I was thinking more of what we said about . . . you know." I dip my head so my hair partially hides my face from him. "About getting married and having a wedding and all of that stuff."

Rhyson's eyes narrow before he speaks.

"You don't want that anymore?" he asks softly, carefully.

"Of course, I do." I smooth my hands over the sheets covering my knees. "I just . . . well, I just wanted to tell you I know building Prodigy takes so much time and effort and energy. I understand that. I don't want you to feel any pressure for that stuff to happen right away. That's all."

It's really quiet, and even though I can't make myself look at him, I feel the weight of his eyes on me. He uses a finger under my chin to turn my head until I can't avoid his eyes.

"Kai, I feel no pressure to do anything."

My stomach free-falls a little. He feels no pressure? Well, dang . . .

"I don't feel pressure to make you my wife," he continues, "Because in my mind, you already are."

Rhyson has this way of allaying my fears and easing my insecurities just by loving me. By telling me what's in his heart. He always seems to have just what I need, whether it's a word or a look. All the doubts that have been wound so tightly inside of me loosen until I'm smiling because I'm sure. I'm sure of him, of us. He smiles back, drops a kiss on my head, and tosses off the sheet, walking tall and naked toward the bathroom.

"Where are you going?" I try not to whine at his abrupt exit, but I probably fail.

"Appointments," he yells. "Most of the day."

But it's my birthday, I wail in my head.

I've never wanted much on my birthdays, but with Rhyson being gone for over a week, I hoped I'd at least have him. I don't need gifts or anything. Just him. And now the only thing I want today is walking out on me. The sound of the shower deflates me.

Rhyson pops his head back into the bedroom, and I fix my face, pulling my pouty bottom lip into a smile.

"Hey, I'm sorry about today," he says. "It's unavoidable stuff, but I want to take you out to dinner for your birthday. Would that be okay?"

We never go out. Not really.

"Like on a date?" I ask, my smile wide and hopeful.

"Yep, like on a date." He widens his eyes. "And no moustaches or disguises!"

"Now that's just crazy talk." I laugh and stretch to retrieve my iPad from the floor. "I'd love that. Thank you."

"What's that you're reading?" Rhyson steps back into the room. He leans against the doorframe and crosses his arms over his broad chest. I have a clear view of the rest of his naked body. The golden slope of his shoulders and the flex of muscles in his stomach. The chiseled slits at his hips. My mouth waters because as exhausted as we were last night, we only made love once before dragging our tired bodies to bed. I'm so hungry for his dick, I'm surprised my stomach doesn't growl.

"Pep? I said what are you reading?"

He keeps a straight face, but I see that glint in his eye. He knows exactly how he's distracting me, especially since I still feel phantom swipes of his tongue between my legs before he abandoned me. I refuse to give him the satisfaction.

"It's a script Bristol wants me to audition for." I clear my throat and jerk my eyes away from the cock that is already half erect between the power of his thighs. "She says the director asked for me specifically."

"What kind of part?" Rhyson scowls. "Is there nudity?

I consider torturing him before shaking my head.

"No." I grin and draw my knees up to my chin, setting the tablet aside. "Not for my part. Not for me."

"Damn right not for you," he mumbles.

"You're such a caveman." I laugh and change the subject before he starts digging too deeply into it, and finds some excuse he doesn't want me to audition. "Where are we going tonight? How should I dress?"

"It's a surprise." He rubs his chin as if thinking about it. "Hmmm. How should you dress? Dress in such a way that when I see you, I'll immediately want to keep you here at home and fuck you all night. Make me regret having to leave the house."

I'm gonna need reinforcements. In my head I'm already formulating my pleas to Ella for assistance.

"I think I can do that."

"Good." He turns toward the bathroom, giving me an unobstructed view of that firm ass. "I need to get out of here. So much to do today."

Disappointment returns, turning my mouth down a little at the corners.

"Hey, Pep," he calls from the bathroom.

"Yeah?" I try to keep my voice light so he doesn't know how much I want him to stay with me in bed for the next eight hours.

"If you hurry up, you can suck my dick and then I'll eat you out and bend you over the counter and fuck you from behind."

I'm tripping over the sheets to get out of bed almost before his last word hits the air.

"Coming!"

4

ai

"MISSION ACCOMPLISHED?" I ASK ELLA, GLIDING my hands over the shantung silk plastered to my body.

"Oh, hell yeah." Ella's wicked, satisfied laugh makes me smile. "He'll definitely want to stay home when he sees you in this dress."

I view myself objectively in the guest bathroom's full-length mirror. Ella and I have been cloistered in here for the last two hours. I didn't want Rhyson to see me until the last minute. I know it's just a date, but it feels special. Not just because it's my birthday. We're not party people. We're as content . . . no, more content . . . staying home. Or going to the studio. Or to the beach. But a date? Dinner? Like normal people? Yeah, I'm excited.

Ella thought it would be fun to play up my Asian ancestry. The shantung silk dress she brought over is the color of cherries and has black piping. It's sleeveless with a stiff mandarin collar framing my neck. High side slits extend from the mid-calf hem to a few inches above my knees, flashing my thighs with each step. The material clings to my every dip and curve. Ella insisted I ditch the bra, so my breasts strain against the tight material. The rear view provides the dress's true drama. A tiny onyx button clasps at my nape, and from there the dress cuts out, laying my entire back bare. The dress lovingly exaggerates and cups the rounded curve of my butt.

Glancing over my shoulder, even I see that it is . . . provocative. Ella knotted my hair and secured it with shiny black chopsticks. My makeup is heavier than usual, with pencil and smoky shadow highlighting the tilt of my eyes. My lips pop a vibrant matte red.

"Kai!" Rhyson's voice climbs the stairs. "Come on, babe. We've got a reservation."

"Be right down," I yell back. Why do we even have intercom when Rhyson always resorts to the old cup and string method of communication?

"Oh!" Ella digs in her little bag of tricks, handing me a small beaded clutch. "You'll need this."

"Thanks, Ella."

"And those." She points to the backless heels on the bed which add a good four inches to my height.

I step into the heels, teetering a little until I get used to the air up here.

"Pep!" Rhyson yells again from downstairs. "Baby, we need to go."

Ella gathers her things and heads toward the landing with me. We're chatting, laughing over something from Grip's shoot, when I catch sight of Rhyson at the bottom of the stairs wearing a slate grey suit with a navy button up, no tie. The slacks are impeccably tailored. He's gotten his hair cut today. Must have been one of his "appointments." It's tapered in the back and on the sides, but still longer on top, dipping into his eyes. He looks like exactly what he is. A devastating famous rock star who can have anyone he wants. If I pinched myself every time I tried to wake up from this dream where I'm the one he wants, I'd be black and blue for the rest of our lives.

I stop right in front of him on the last step, which between my high heels and the elevation of the step, puts us basically eye to eye. We stare at one another for long moments, his eyes thoroughly assessing me, and mine doing the same. Ella says her good-byes, and I wave vaguely in her direction, transfixed by Rhyson's stormy gaze. Finally he grabs my hand, draws my wrist to his lips and leaves a sweet kiss there.

"Well, I hope you're happy," he says softly, making another journey up and then down my body with his eyes. "You did it."

"Did what?" I'm startled by how husky and breathless I sound.

"You've made me want to stay home and say screw our plans."

"It's my birthday." I lean in to plant a kiss on his full lips, barely resisting the impulse to thrust my tongue in and set off some fireworks. "And remember, reservations."

I step down and walk past him. His indrawn breath once he sees the back of the dress renders a pleased smile on my face. My hand is on the door handle when his wide palm splays over my stomach, pulling me up short. His hard chest warms my back.

"Your ass in this dress is obscene, Pep," he husks at my ear, grinding his erection into my butt. I'm reminded of my own cries bouncing off the bathroom walls this morning when he took me from behind as we watched each other in the mirror.

I glance up and over my shoulder, giving him my most seductive smile and turn to face him.

"I know."

He brushes his thumbs over the undersides of my breasts through the silk before sliding his hands over my ribs.

"If we didn't have plans," he says, fitting his palms to the curve of my hips. "I'd take you right here."

"But we do." I peer up through the heavy mascara of my lashes. "Right?"

Even with it being my birthday, part of me wishes he'd say we'll cancel our reservations and do just that.

"Later," I whisper, my eyes never straying from his face.

He leans into me for a kiss that goes deep and quick before he forces himself back with a groan.

"Later," he repeats with one last incendiary look as he opens the door, pressing his hand to the small of my bare back. "I'm gonna hold you to that."

As long as he's holding me.

5

Kai

"SO YOU HAVE A THING FOR Porsches, huh?"

Rhyson grins, keeping his eyes trained on the road without replying. I knew he had a few other cars in that warehouse of a garage, but he never drives anything but the Cayenne. I had no idea what a Panamera even was until he opened the door for me to slide into the silver sedan's passenger seat. If power screwed luxury up against a wall and made an auto baby, this car would be it. My fingers caress the supple scarlet leather. It must be stitched with sex threads because I have to rub my legs together like cricket wings to tamp down the arousal of the car purring through the seat beneath me.

Everything about tonight feels . . . rich and decadent. For one, we're alone. Gep nor anyone from the security team accompanies us. Our intimacy, our aloneness is worth more than diamonds to me. The costly dress caressing my hips and legs feels rich. The raw silk licking over my braless nipples. The outrageous satin thong Rhyson bought for me a few weeks ago is the only thing tiny enough to wear under this tight dress. Even the early summer air, losing its cloying thickness the longer we drive, feels as light and clear as champagne.

"So where are we going?" I probe.

We've been driving for twenty minutes and he's barely said a word. I'm unfamiliar with this Rhyson, distracted and tightly wound. His energy, coiled into a figure-eight knot, permeates the car's interior, but none of it is focused on me. He's completely in his head. I've gotten spoiled by his undivided attention. Maybe his "appointments" didn't go well today.

"Rhys? Did you hear me?"

"Sorry." He turns his head long enough to catch my eyes. "What'd you say?"

"Where are we going?" I slow my speech as if he needs to read my lips.

"I told you it's a surprise." A smile quirks his mouth. "You'll see soon enough."

"How'd your appointments go today?" I ask, not wanting to sink back into the silence where his mind is elsewhere.

"Fine." His voice remains neutral, but a smile I can only describe as secretive curves on his lips. "We're here."

"Here" is Tide, a Pacific-side restaurant nestled against the curving California coastline. Extremely popular, and judging by the queue of cars snaking from the entrance, packed. There's a flurry of activity as we approach, with patrons leaving their cars and valets hopping in to drive off and make room for more. My eyes swing to Rhyson's and find him already watching me.

"What do you think?" For the first time since we left the house, I have his full attention. His eyes are trained on my face, watching closely for my reaction.

"It's gorgeous." I look back to the restaurant's glass paneled walls offering shadowy glimpses of the ocean view. "Crowded. You know everyone comes here, right?"

"Right." With a satisfied nod, he gets out so the valet can take the car.

An attendant opens my door and offers me a hand.

"I've got her," Rhyson says, inserting himself between me and the eager valet.

I step out, and Rhyson's eyes drop to the indecent length of leg the panels of my dress fall back to display. "I love this dress, Pep, but it's a hazard. I'm hoping to get through the night without punching some ogling idiot in the face."

I tip up a few inches to kiss him, but remember where we are. Rhyson and I aren't that couple who do pubic displays of affection. We save all our passion for behind closed doors. A few paps have caught us holding hands and snapped a picture here and there, but not much more than that. By design. I'm pulling back when Rhyson grips my hips, bringing me back to my tiptoes. His mouth slants over mine in pure possession, one hand palming the curve of my ass while the other slides over the naked skin of my back. He juts into my mouth, searching for my tongue, and we groan at the taste of each other. My heart slams against his through our chests, and my hand drifts up his neck and into his hair. My fingers curl compulsively into the heavy, thick waves. I want him so badly. I need him more than air. I love him beyond all my girlish imaginations. I forget for just a few moments that we are surrounded by people and inevitably cameras. A flash over his shoulder punctures my haze and reminds me that we aren't alone.

"Rhys," I whisper against his lips, putting a few inches between us. "Someone just took our picture."

He leans down to give me another kiss, unchecked and hungry.

"Good."

Well, okay. I missed the PDA memo, but if he's fine with it then so am I.

He enfolds my hand in his and leads me toward the door framed by majestic trees wrapped in lights. As he gives his name, unnecessarily of course, to the elegantly dressed Amazon at the podium, I can't help but notice how her eyes covet him from head to toe. Admittedly, he is beautiful, but it's more than that. Rhyson could wear a bag over his head and still draw every eye in the room. His energy, the latent charisma that he turns on and off at will, compels you to watch because you aren't sure when you'll meet someone like him again. I want to tell the Amazon to get a room before she fucks someone with her eyes that way. My lips tighten and my eyes narrow at the edges. I don't want to be that jealous girl, insecure because her famous boyfriend has more opportunity to cheat than most men would ever dream of. I glance at Rhyson to see if he even notices. His eyes are clinging to me, and he smiles knowingly. He bends down to caress my ear with his lips.

"Only you, Pep."

A breath stutters past my lips. I can't look away from him and can't stop smiling. He knows me so well. He took the time to know me. We take the time to know one another, and I wouldn't trade our friendship, the cornerstone of this love affair, for any gift he could ever give me.

"This way, Mr. Gray." The Amazon leads us with a sway of her generous hips through the crowded main dining room and down a long corridor. The dimly lit hall seems to crack open with light all of a sudden when we reach the outdoor deck. I'm so captivated by the sky tipping into sunset over the vast ocean like a painter's palette that I don't even notice all the people crowding the deck until they scream.

"Surprise!"

I've always wondered why people's hands fly to their mouths. Why their fingers touch their chests when they're blown away. Now I know. There's so much delight, so much completely unexpected happiness that swells up inside of you, you just want to contain it. You don't want to leak any of it, so you cover your mouth to hold it in. You press it back into your chest when it feels like it might explode from you.

A startled little laugh whooshes out of me. Everyone is here, laughing as they realize they really did "get me," and I had no clue.

San, who was supposed to be on assignment in Turks and Caicos, stands near the front of the crowd, ear-to-ear grin plastered all over his face. Bristol, Grip, Grady, Em, Ella, Luke, Gep, and the security team cluster together. Even Amber, the receptionist from Wood, and all of the studio engineers are here. No way. Even my friend Misty from The Note. A few faces are less familiar, and I recognize them as friends and associates of Rhyson's. So many friends. So many faces. And then I stumble upon one precious face, and the tears, which have been cooperating by just standing in my eyes, leak over my cheeks.

"Aunt Ruthie?" I gasp and rush toward the woman who has anchored me through the roughest storms of my life. She does what she always does—she catches me. Her arms encircle and nearly squeeze the life out of me. I pull back to look at her face and touch the hair that keeps on greying and she keeps on refusing to dye.

"As I live and breathe." I laugh through my tears. "You're in LA. What are you doing here?"

"Well, it is your birthday, and I heard there was gonna be a party." Her blue eyes warm between the fine lines fanning out over the lightly freckled skin. "B'sides, a handsome young man flies to the sticks to get you in a private plane. How can an old bird like me resist?"

"Rhyson came to get you?" Confusion creases a frown on my face. "When? When did he come?"

"Last night. I have to get back to Glory Bee tomorrow, but he'll get me home." Aunt Ruthie smiles over my shoulder. "Thanks again for the lift."

I glance up and behind me to see Rhyson standing right there, grinning back at Aunt Ruthie. His hands settle, warm and possessive, at my waist and draw me back into his chest.

"Last night?" I twist around to search his face. "But I thought . . . but you . . . huh?"

"The extra day was for the flight to Glory Falls. Had to pick up some precious cargo." He squeezes my sides lightly. "Surprised?"

I swallow back emotion scorching the inside of my throat. I wondered why he took an extra day in New York. I pouted over him spending today of all days on his "appointments" instead of with me. I resented not having his full attention all the way here, and apparently . . . it was all for me. All to make this birthday this special.

"I can't believe you did all this." I hook my arms behind his neck, straining up and into him. "Thank you."

He tightens his hands at my waist, easily lifting until my feet aren't quite on the ground anymore.

"I wish every day was your birthday," he whispers over my lips. "It'd give me an excuse to show you what you mean to me all the time."

A man this closed off from most people, a man with so little reason to trust, opens himself to me every day and trusts me with everything he owns. Trusts me with his home and his heart. And yes, even though he may not be hearing wedding bells quite yet, he trusts me with his future. It overwhelms me, the privilege of his love. And even with Aunt Ruthie right behind me and dozens of eyes on us, I don't even care. I wriggle closer to him, wind my fingers in the cool strands of his hair and capture his lips between mine. And it's not a cute kiss. It's ravishment, a battle waged with lips and teeth and tongue. As glad as I am to have all our friends here, I couldn't care less if everyone else just walked right off into the glorious sunset and left me and this man to celebrate alone in each other's arms.

He laughs against my lips, slowly dripping my body down the front of his until my stilettos touch the floor again.

"Damn, Pep." His voice is husky and a small smile rests on lips faintly red with my lipstick. Lust lingers in his eyes. "Save some for later."

I laugh a little self-consciously and wipe the lipstick from his mouth. I start to pull away, but Rhyson bends to whisper in my ear, holding me still in front of him.

"You might, uh, wanna just stand here for a second unless you want this boner poking Aunt Ruthie in the eye."

I drop my head to his chest and giggle, but stand there obediently until he releases me to greet the people waiting to wish me a happy birthday.

It's a beautiful night in every way. Candles and champagne flutes grace a long wooden table draped with linen. Steak and seafood and fresh vegetables and luscious fruit lay heavy on the plates at each seat. Lights wrap around the trees sprouting right up through the wooden deck floor, embracing the trunks and sprinkling through the leaves that canopy our celebration. I'm stuffed and happy, eating the delicious food, chatting and laughing with people as they come by where I sit with Rhyson, our hands linked under the table.

"Did you both know about this?" I split a look of mock censure between Bristol and Ella.

"Yes," they answer in unison, laughing.

"I thought I would bust helping you get ready for tonight," Ella admits. "When you called and asked me to come over, I just knew I wouldn't be able to keep the secret all afternoon."

"I never suspected." I glance at Bristol. "And you never let on either."

"We were sworn to secrecy under threat of death." Bristol nods to Rhyson beside me. "He wouldn't let me do anything. He wanted to handle everything himself. Good job, brother."

Rhyson glances at me with a small smile and then away.

"And you're the worst at keeping secrets, San." I punch him in the shoulder, seated beside me. "I can't believe you never let on. Were you ever even in Turks?"

"Yeah." San takes a sip of his white wine. "Gotta be back tomorrow. Rhyson flew me in just for the night."

"For the night?" I turn a surprised glance to Rhyson. "Just for my birthday? Wow."

"Did you save room for cake?" Rhyson doesn't acknowledge his extravagance.

A server carrying a multi-tiered pink and white cake lit with sparkler candles walks out onto the deck. Everyone starts singing

"Happy Birthday" right on cue. The whole scene—the starry sky, the illuminated trees, the crescendo of crashing waves, the crowd of eager faces—grows blurry through new tears. It's just so much and so perfect.

"Blow out the candles!"

Though my chest feels tight, I draw in what I hope is enough breath to extinguish all these candles. My lips are puckered and poised, when Rhyson presses a staying hand to my shoulder.

"Don't forget to make a wish." He kisses my forehead softly and then nods to the cake.

I must be a selfish, hard-to-please girl. With all of this tonight, with every dream I ever had for my career becoming a reality, with all of these people who care about me, I shouldn't want another thing. But there is a wish that hides in my heart. I conceal it. I tell it to wait. Most days, I pretend it isn't there. But today, when I'm given permission to hope, to pray, to dream, to wish—I do. I draw the force of that buried wish up from my belly, through my chest and blow as hard as I can until every candle goes dark.

Just in case wishes come true.

I'm polishing off my mammoth slice of white chocolate cake when Rhyson touches my wrist lightly to get my attention.

"I think cake is your weakness. I seem to remember you devouring it once before."

Something wicked kindles in his eyes. It takes a moment before I remember the last time he saw me stuffing my face with cake. At Grady and Em's wedding. It was my first time seeing him since our fight over the Total Package fiasco. I can almost smell the hay in that loft where he laid me down and eased my dress up. Can almost feel his hands caressing behind my knees and his fingers incinerating the sensitive skin inside my thighs. The memory of his tongue licking hungrily into my pussy and the way his moans vibrated against my clit enflames my cheeks.

"You tasted better than the cake," he whispers, brushing his thumb secretly, subtly over my nipple. "If I think about it long enough, I still taste you in my mouth."

"Rhyson!" I hiss, glancing around at everyone around us who seems occupied with their cake and conversations.

"I can't wait to get you home and out of this dress so I can taste you again." His words waft over my flushed skin like steam. "It's all I've thought about since you walked down those stairs."

I nod numbly, not even trying to deny that I want it too. I need it too. His words, the hot looks, the covert touches have all aroused a fire in me hot enough to ignite the tiny thong I'm wearing.

"Wanna dance?" He extends his hand casually like he wasn't just seducing me with his suggestions. Like he asks me this every day.

"With who?" I shove aside my lust with a little laugh at my own joke. "You don't dance, remember? And besides, there's no . . ."

I trail off as music starts lightly piping in through the hidden speakers. Rhyson stands up and extends his hand to me, waiting. I can't tell if he's just resigned or eager or what, but something weird is going on with his face. He hates dancing. We never dance together, and he obviously looks forward to the prospect about as much as a colonoscopy. So why would he even ask?

"We don't have to, Rhys. Really."

"No, I want to." He takes the choice away and tugs me to the center of the patio. "Don't get used to this. It's a one-time offer."

"Well, I'll take it." I lay my head on his chest, stiffening a little when I realize we're the only ones on the floor. "Rhys, no one else is dancing."

"That's because it's our night." His lips move against my hair.

I'm processing that when the music playing penetrates my senses.

"Is that 'Lost'?" I grin up at him and link my fingers behind his neck. "They're playing our song."

"One of them, yeah." He grins a little, but that look is back, the weird one, before he masks it with the self-assured expression I've grown used to. "When you first told me this was your favorite song from my album, it solidified what I already knew."

I can vividly recall our conversation in his car the first time we hung out. We talked about "Lost," the song that was like a light in a dark forest when I had to stay behind in Glory Falls and take care of Mama.

"And what did you already know?" I tease him with a smile, reaching up to curl my fingers in his hair.

"That you were special." His eyes don't tease me back. There's a warm sobriety there that melts the smile from my face. "I think on some level, I knew even then we were supposed to be together. Hell, I think I knew that the first time I saw you and we hadn't even spoken one word."

"Love at first sight, huh?" I try to make my tone light again, but this moment gets weightier and weightier the longer he stares back at me.

"Not love. Not at first." He shakes his head and links our hands on his chest. "But a recognition of sorts. I think my soul knew you before I did. Knew you were the one I should spend the rest of my life with. Getting to know you, becoming your friend, only convinced me of what I think my heart and my soul already knew."

"And what's that?" I ask, my voice raspy with the emotion this conversation evokes.

"That you're mine and I'm yours." His smile is so tender and warm that it burns away the periphery until I don't see anyone else; don't even care anymore that we are the only ones in the center of the patio dancing.

"This morning you so thoughtfully relieved me of any pressure to make things . . . shall we say 'official' between us." His hand slides down and tightens at my hip, slowing the swaying of our bodies until we're standing still. "And I told you I felt no pressure to make you my wife because to me you already are."

"I know. It's fine, Rhyson. Like I said, there's a lot going on. You don't have to explain. I'm fine the way we are, baby."

"But I'm not." He presses his forehead to mine, splaying his palms across my back to inch me closer until there's nothing between us but a breath of balmy summer air. "I want the whole world to know we're together forever. To know when they see me, they see you. To know that what's mine belongs to you. That I'm yours. To know that our lives are linked till death do us part. And even beyond that."

I don't know what he's saying. Or why he's saying it now. Here. I spare a quick glance around the deck, a little embarrassed to see that most people have stopped talking and are watching us closely.

"I want them to know tonight." He steps back just a little and then drops in front of me. "I want you to know tonight."

My legs liquefy and my head swims seeing him down on one knee. This moment, the one I wished for when I blew out my candles but didn't think would come this soon or this way, sucks all the air from my chest like a vacuum. I must sway a little because he steadies me at my waist with one strong hand. I look down at his face, the one I wasn't even sure was handsome at first, but now is so beautiful to me I can't imagine waking up with anyone else for the rest of my days. He stares back at me with such love that the next words out of his mouth are almost unnecessary because his eyes are already asking me the question and my heart has already answered.

"Kai, would you do me the honor of becoming something I wasn't even sure I would ever want?" A slow, certain smile curves his full lips. "My wife. Will you marry me?"

And as much as my heart utters yes. As much as my body screams its agreement. As much as my soul says amen, I can't get the word out. It's stuck in my throat. Trapped by emotion and the enormity of all my wishes convening in this one man and coming impossibly true.

"I know this isn't how you probably thought it would happen," he rushes to say. "I mean with all these people watching, but the whole world got to witness the lowest point in our relationship. On that video they got to see that fight, the day I almost ruined everything. I wanted the whole world to see this too. To see that I choose you. There's no one else for me. Only you, Pep."

My eyes wander around the circle of people watching. San, who stood with me by my mother's grave and convinced me to come to LA, wears a satisfied smile. Ella is wiping tears from her cheeks. Bristol looks suspiciously bright-eyed. Grip wears the biggest "that's my boy" grin. Grady looks . . . proud. The proudest I've ever seen him. Aunt Ruthie's small smile widens when I meet her eyes.

"How long you gonna keep that man on his knees, Kai Anne?" Aunt Ruthie yells with hands cupped around her lips, soliciting laughter from everyone standing around waiting for my response.

A shaky laugh slips past my lips, and I swipe at the tears trickling over my own cheeks. When I look back to Rhyson he doesn't look worried about the wait. His eyes hold the complete confidence of a man who is about to be told yes, today and for the rest of his life. Of a man whose soul is so completely tangled around mine, that I'm sure his heart already hears my response. He's right. In so many ways, this is just a formality acknowledging something to the world that we've known for a long time. I'm his and he's mine. We don't need a ceremony to confirm that, but when I notice for the first time that he's holding a ring, I physically feel my jaw coming unhinged. It's so gorgeous and so perfect. The square-cut sapphire ring, orbited by diamonds of such purity, steals my breath. I don't know carats or cuts. I have no idea how much it costs, but I do know, as I extend my hand and he slides the glorious thing home on my finger, that I will wear it until I die.

"You still haven't said yes." Rhyson kisses the ring on my finger, his eyes amused, but drenched with emotion.

I can't stand it another second. Everything that was shocked into silence, every trapped breath, every frozen tear, breaks free all at once. And I'm laughing. I'm hyperventilating. I'm crying. I'm sliding down to my knees on the wooden floor with him, tight dress and high heels and all, hooking my arms behind his neck and laying my temple against his chin.

"Yes, Rhyson."

I look up at him and don't even try to wipe the tears away anymore because this is the most singularly spectacular moment of my life. No number one album, no Grammy, no tour, nothing will ever come close to the day he invited me to spend the rest of my life with him. I tuck my head into the scent, the warmth of his neck.

"God, yes. Of course yes."

6

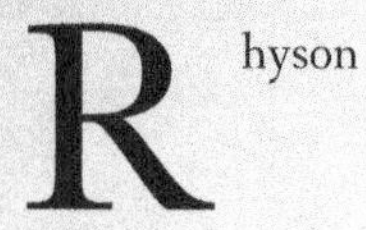

hyson

I HAVEN'T HEARD THE LAST FIVE minutes of what Bristol said. Not that this meeting isn't important. Of course it is. The artist showcase in Vegas next week is a huge deal for Prodigy. It's pivotal for Marlon's upcoming debut album. It's Luke's first performance as a Prodigy artist, and a great opportunity to widen his fan base. It will help Kilimanjaro continue the transition from underground indie to mainstream. So it's important, but I can barely focus because I'm so distracted by my fiancée sitting across the table from me.

Kai looks beautiful today. Pretty much like every other day. She's scooped her hair up into a slouchy bun, and soft tendrils curl around her neck. Her face is completely bare except for a slick of lip gloss. She's wearing a Janet Jackson Control tour tank top and dark wash skinny jeans with flip flops. Even though I completely emptied myself inside her only an hour ago, I want to peel her clothes off and spread her on Prodigy's glass conference room table. I'd push her knees back and dip my head between those legs . . . anddddd . . . I'm hard again.

Fuck.

Fiancée.

I find an excuse to say it at least twenty times a day, but it never gets old. Even I didn't realize how seeing Kai wearing my ring would affect me. I nearly had an aneurysm choosing the damn thing. I changed my mind four times before deciding on the sapphire. Literally took three rings back and didn't pick it up until the morning of the party. One of my appointments. I'm probably banned at Neil Lane. No, as much as I spent on that ring, I'm thinking they'd still welcome me with open arms. It was completely worth the years I shaved off my life finding the perfect one. I think she likes it. Actually I know she loves it. Even now she's staring at it with a kind of dazed look on her face, which cracks me up.

"Earth to Kai." Bristol, standing at the head of the table, shifts her weight from one foot to the other, placing a fist on her hip. "If you could stop gawking at that ginormous ring for five seconds and pay attention, that'd be totally awesome."

Kai's wide eyes flick up from her ring finger to Bristol's half-amused, half-irate face.

"Sorry, guys."

She offers an apologetic glance to Luke and Marlon, who sit at the conference table, and to the guys from Kilimanjaro on the flat screen who Skyped in. Her eyes finally settle on me, and a goofy grin overtakes her face. The last week has been . . . God, like a Disney movie. Like birds singing, the-hills-are-alive kind of sappy happy. I'm deliriously disgusted with myself. Not nearly as disgusted as my twin sister is with me and my . . . fiancée.

"Look, I was there," Bristol says. "It was magical. The party, the engagement, the tweets and Instagram. The whole world is gushing about it. I get it, but I need you to focus so we can make sure we're all on the same page for next week's showcase."

She bends an exasperated look on me.

"'All' means you, too, Rhyson."

"I heard everything you said." I inject more confidence in my voice than I actually feel on the subject. "Luke will go first and perform four songs from his last album. Kilimanjaro will do a couple of songs from their last EP. Marlon'll use tracks for the songs he's featured on and a live band for his own stuff. Bam."

"And your part?" Bristol tilts her head. "Did you hear that?"

"Well, let's talk about it," I say as a non-answer since, no, I checked out on that part.

"The organizers want you to close the show, on piano preferably." Bristol shuffles through a stack of papers in front of her, eyes and attention held by something else. "Just a couple songs."

"I'm not the artist here." I frown and massage the hand in my lap. "Let's just focus on these guys at the showcase. The public's still getting to know them. They already know me."

"That's the point." Bristol angles a look at me like I should know this. "You're the sure bet. They're meeting everyone else. I mean, yeah, Luke and Grip have been out there for the last year or so, but everyone's gonna want to hear and see you too, Rhys. Especially now that we've delayed your next album."

"Not this time." I flatten my mouth into the stubborn line to match Bristol's. "Just these guys for Vegas."

"It's actually not an option." Bristol's silvery eyes, so much like mine, show a little caution for the first time. "That was non-negotiable. The organizers want you, Rhyson. Of course they do."

"When was that non-negotiable negotiated?" My words tumble out hot in the air-conditioned conference room. "Did I miss a conversation where you asked me what the hell I wanted to do, Bris?"

It's completely quiet for a moment. I know it's irrational. I've been playing the piano longer than I've known how to read. This should be no big deal. I sense Marlon's confusion, Bristol's irritation, and Kilimanjaro's discomfort. And Kai? When I look at her across the table, her brows clip together, and her eyes rest on my left hand rubbing my right. I immediately push both hands through my hair.

"Let's see if we can get that changed." I avoid Kai's sharp eyes in favor of my twin's annoyed ones.

"Can you and I discuss this offline?" Bristol huffs a quick sigh. "Let's talk about Kai before we break."

"What are we thinking?" I risk a glance at Kai, but her concerned eyes still rest on my hand.

Dammit.

"Well, she has the duet with Luke that you wrote, so she could come on during his set and perform with him." Bristol glances down at her iPad. "And then she and Grip have 'How You Like It' popping off soon. We could cap his set with that one."

"That sounds good." I glance at Kai, who nods her agreement, but questions still cloud her dark eyes when she looks at me.

"And, well, I did have another thought." Bristol clears her throat. There's never anything actually in my sister's throat to clear. That's her tell when something makes her uncomfortable.

"A thought, huh?" I tip my chair away from the long glass conference table and link my hands behind my head. "Let's hear it."

"Well, it's hard to ignore that the video Kai did with Luke is one of the most watched clips on YouTube. Millions of hits." Bristol squares her shoulders and looks at me directly. "With dance being such a huge part of who Kai is as an artist, we could be missing an opportunity not having her perform the . . . um, the dance she did in Luke's video and on tour."

She means the fucking lap dance.

"No." I crumple the word into a dismissal and toss it in Bristol's face. "What else ya got?"

"Rhyson, we should at least discuss—"

"No, Bristol." I turn the full force of my refusal on her. "Hell no. She's not doing that fucking lap dance again."

"Let's just consider it," Bristol presses while everyone else averts their eyes, coughs and finds something fascinating on their phones. "I want to make sure we give her enough stage time."

"Okay. Instead of having her pop into Luke and Marlon's set," I argue. "Let them pop into her set. We'll do their two songs and an onstage interview with her."

"I like that." Marlon nods and smiles at Kai.

"She could do songs from the set she used to open my tour," Luke suggests, his eyes affectionate when he looks at Kai. They grew really close on tour, like brother and sister. I know it's no more than that, and Luke would never lobby for the lap dance. It's disrespectful to me and to my relationship with Kai. Everyone at this table knows that, except Bristol apparently. And if she doesn't back down, she'll force me to put her in her place in front of everybody.

"This isn't that big of a deal. The dance could—" Bristol starts.

"Just the two songs with Marlon and Luke," I say, barreling over whatever nonsense she was about to suggest. "That's the end of it."

"Only two songs?" Bristol glances at Kai's blank expression.

"I don't want you doing a bunch of covers." I gentle my tone some when I address Kai. "Let's stick with only original content. We're still defining you as part of the Prodigy family and as an artist in your own right."

"But—" Bristol starts.

"No buts," I counter before Bristol can finish. "I don't want to overexpose Kai when we're still shaping her brand. Her debut album isn't even in production yet, much less released."

"Well, she has movie offers and endorsement deals stacking up," Bristol says, her smile slightly smug. "So you'll have to get past that overexposure thing."

"Movies and endorsements?" I look at Kai, who glances between Bristol and me uneasily. "What's she talking about, Pep?"

Before Kai can answer, Bristol butts in . . . again.

"Several, and I got a few more this morning."

"Well, I told you about the script." Kai shuffles her eyes between my sister and me. "Endorsements?"

"You still haven't checked your email?" A touch of impatience pinches Bristol's expression. "We talked about this."

"I know." Kai grabs her phone and slides her finger over the screen. "I finally got all my stuff set up on this new phone."

"Well, Grip and Luke, you guys know what next week looks like." I shift a glance to the flat screen where Kilimanjaro joins us from Seattle. "Guys, you have any questions?"

"Nah, we're good," Nate the lead singer assures me.

"Is that all for them, Bristol?" I ask.

"Yeah." Bristol runs a hand over her sleek ponytail. "We'll make sure your managers and assistants have itineraries and details for the trip."

She lasers a sharp look at Marlon, fake frowning.

"Oh, wait." Bristol rifles through her papers again. "Grip, I don't seem to have your manager's info here. Surely you have a team by now?"

"Like I told you, contracts go to my agent." Marlon's dark eyes crinkle at the edges with the grin he shoots her way. "Just send the details to me until I find the right person to manage me."

"Some people always miss the good thing standing right in front of them." Bristol tsks and shakes her head.

"I couldn't agree more." He stands up, putting him close enough to tower over her. Their eyes catch and hold, crackling the air around them.

What the hell have I missed?

"So . . . we're done?" I ask, catching Marlon's suddenly serious eyes. He glances at Bristol one last time before nodding and grabbing his bag from the floor.

"Um, yeah." Bristol takes a step back, putting a few more inches between her and Marlon. "Thanks, guys."

Bristol slips her iPad into its sleeve and slings a leather bag over her shoulder.

"Not you, Bris. You and Kai stay."

As soon as the door closes behind Marlon, I go in.

"What endorsement deals? What movie offers?"

Bristol wordlessly digs out a folder and slides it across the table to me. When I open it, there's printed emails from six, seven, eight companies inquiring about using Kai to represent their brands, everything from shampoo to leotards. On the last page, Bristol has compiled a list of movie projects submitted for Kai's consideration. When did all of this happen? Bristol's only been representing Kai for a few weeks.

"I mean, Kai's been featured on a couple of songs, yeah. She opened for Luke's tour and was in his video, but all this?" I rest my elbows on the table, leaning forward. "I'm just surprised there's this much . . ."

"Interest?" Bristol prompts.

"Well, yeah." I glance at Kai, hoping I'm not offending her. "We all know how amazing she is, but this seems like a lot for the little the public has seen so far."

"Rhyson, you aren't that naïve." Kai looks away from me to tap and slide over her phone screen, her voice tightening. "You know why there's so much interest."

"She's right." Bristol flops into a seat beside Kai.

"Huh?" I shake my head. "Enlighten me."

"You," Kai says softly. She looks up from the emails she's sorting through. "They're interested in me because of you."

Well, shit. That's the last thing I want. And I know it's the last thing Kai ever wanted.

"It's true." Bristol shrugs. "Everyone knows Kai's talented, but there wouldn't be anywhere near this level of interest if she weren't dating you. Correction, engaged to you. It is what it is. I say we maximize it."

"Of course you say that." My sister and I glare at each other for a moment, like warring mirrors. "What about you, Kai? What do you think?"

"Huh?" She looks down at her screen before refocusing on me. "I'm sorry. I need to go make a quick call."

"What's wrong, babe?" I frown because she's frowning.

"I'd just been thinking for days I forgot to do something, and just realized what it was." She stands and speedwalks toward the door. "I'll be right back."

"Don't do this again, Rhys." Bristol levels a hard look at me once Kai's gone.

"Do what?"

"This thing where you try to control Kai and her career. Just let us handle it. Let her make the decisions for herself."

Am I doing that again? I started family therapy at Kai's request. I didn't expect to gain much from it except to prove to her how serious I was about addressing my issues. Except . . . now I actually am addressing my issues. I still need a sweater to be in the same room with my own mother because things remain so cold between us, but things have thawed significantly with my father. Dr. Ramirez has helped us a lot. There are two questions she always encourages me to ask myself when I'm sorting through things. Why am I really feeling this way? Have I felt this way before?

When I use those questions to test my feelings about what Kai should do with these offers, I know. I feel this way, not because I want to control her, but because I honestly believe what I'm saying. Not as the man who loves her and believes the only way I can safeguard our relationship is through control, that controlling her is loving her. But as the man who's been in this industry basically my entire life and has seen how artists in the game for the long term build their brand. And it's not based on who they're dating.

"Look, the public's fascination is notoriously fleeting and fickle." I look at my sister frankly. "Could we accept every opportunity they throw Kai's way? Make sure she's seen in as many places as possible? Saturate? Sure. But I think we have to be more strategic than that. We should focus on getting quality songs and producers for her first album, shoring up any vocal weaknesses with this new voice instructor I want her to try, and finding the right acting coach to prepare her. When she appears in her first movie, I want people to be blown away, not categorizing her as some chick who got a part because of who she's engaged to or because she looks the way she does. Kai's too good for that. Her foundation goes deep. We should build on that, not on public interest tied to me. She can stand on her own. She should stand on her own. I'm not just saying that as the guy lucky enough to be marrying her, but as the one leading this thing. I believe that's the right thing for Kai. I believe it's the right thing for Prodigy, and I'll tell her so myself."

"You just did," Kai says from the door, her voice softened and a smile teasing her lips. "And thank you, Rhyson, for saying all of that. For believing in me."

I don't know how much of my diatribe she heard, but it doesn't matter. I meant every word. I'm not biased in thinking Kai is the best thing since sliced bread. Her career, like anyone else's, if not handled properly, can get off track before it's even begun. I love her too much to let that happen.

"I'll defer to you two lovebirds then." Bristol laughs good-naturedly, standing up again. "I'll just keep taking the offers, bringing them to you, and you can decide."

Kai and I share a smile, and I've never wanted to be someone's partner so badly. Not just in business, in rocketing her career over the next few years, but in life. I want to share every aspect of my life with her, and for her to know when she shares every aspect of hers with me, I'll always act in her best interest.

"See you, Bristol," Kai says as Bristol leaves the office. She looks back to me, and the frown she wore when she left the conference room comes back. "Hey, can one of the guys drive me somewhere?"

"What do you need?" I walk over and slip my arms around her slim frame. "I can take you."

"Um, okay. I thought you might have stuff to do." She draws a quick breath and looks up at me. "My doctor had a cancellation, but I need to leave like right now."

"Doctor?" I tip up her chin to search her eyes and make sure she's not hiding anything from me. "Everything okay?"

"Yeah." She gives me a smile that I don't quite buy. "I kept feeling like I was forgetting something. I realized I missed a doctor's appointment."

"Is that a big deal?" I spread my hand at the small of her back.

"They can squeeze me in today, so it shouldn't be."

Then why does she look like it is?

7

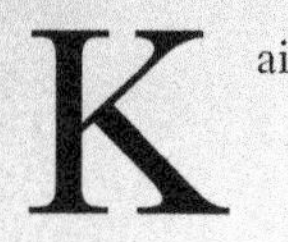

ai

I ALWAYS FEEL LIKE I HAVE these little paper gowns on backward. Is this right? Sitting on the examination table, I peer down at my breasts and panties peeking through the open panels. I can't believe I did this. How did I miss this appointment? I mean, I know how it happened. The tour. My collapse. Our vacation to Bora Bora. The new phone and my screwed up calendar alerts. I've had a lot going on, but to let my birth control shot lapse? And by five weeks?

While I was reading through the offers and projects Bristol sent me, I noticed an email all the way at the bottom of the pile about my missed doctor's appointment. If I'd had my old phone, I would have gotten the reminder call. I would have seen the appointment alert. But I didn't. And now Rhyson and I have been having unprotected sex for the last five weeks.

The hormone stays in your system for a while. I'm sure I've

dodged the bullet. I haven't had any symptoms. No fatigue or morning sickness. Nothing to indicate anything will come from this oversight except a lesson learned. It can't. I tell myself all these things as I sit and wait for the doctor to come in. I'm so close to doing all the things I've always wanted to do. What are the odds that something else will slow me down? That through my own negligence, I will slow myself down?

My phone lights up beside me on the table.

Rhyson: Everything okay? Has the doctor seen you yet?

I smile and dial him.

"Hey," he answers right away.

"Hey. I peed in a cup and the nurse took my blood pressure." I swing my legs hanging over the table's side. "So just waiting for the doctor. What are you doing?"

"Working on some tracks for Kilimanjaro." I hear him still clicking away on the keys while we talk. "There's a song they've been doing on the festival circuit that could be great for their album, but needed some tweaks."

"Cool. Thanks for bringing me. I'm sure you had better things to do than sit in a waiting room full of women. Is anyone giving you trouble?"

"Nah." He chuckles and lowers his voice. "I did have one elderly lady tell me I looked a lot like that folk singer Rhyson Gray."

"Folk singer?" I bend at the waist to laugh, clutching the maybe-backward panels together over my naked chest. "What are you, John Denver now?"

"A few people recognized me and asked for autographs, but it hasn't been that bad. I'm wearing my cap."

"Which is, in your mind at least, like a cloak of invisibility."

"You can't deny its effectiveness."

"Oh, yes, I . . ." My words peter out when the door opens and Dr. Allister walks in. "My doctor just came in, babe. I'll be out soon."

"K. Love you."

"Love you too." I smile at the doctor and bite my lip. "Sorry. I know I'm not supposed to be on my phone. Just checking on my fiancé out in the waiting room."

"Rhyson Gray is in our waiting room?" Dr. Allister's eyes light up behind her blue-rimmed eyeglasses. "He may need a security escort to get out. Our receptionist is a huge fan. Would he like to wait in a private room? Would that be easier for him?"

I process that she knows who I am, and therefore knows who my fiancé is before answering her question.

"He's fine, but I'd like to get this shot so he can leave before people start posting pictures of him to Instagram."

Dr. Allister's smile fades a little. She takes the seat facing the table at the end with the dreaded stirrups.

"Kai, about your shot." She glances down at her clipboard and then back to me, watching me carefully. "You do realize you were overdue, right?"

"Yeah. I was on tour and out of town and then got a new phone." I wave my hand to dismiss all my excuses. "Sorry. You don't want to hear all that. Yes. I was a little past due."

"Five, almost six weeks, past due." Dr. Allister licks her lips and leans forward. "It's standard for us to do a pregnancy test before administering the birth control shot."

The fear I'd barely allowed myself to consider stares back fully-formed at me from behind Dr. Allister's shiny lenses.

"No." I grip the little paper gown in my fist until I'm sure I'll tear it "I'm not . . ."

"Pregnant, yes." Dr. Allister's kind eyes run over my face, which must be drained of all blood.

"But the hormone—"

"The efficacy of the hormone is drastically reduced after even two weeks past the shot, much less nearly six, Kai."

"I just . . . I didn't . . ."

I run a trembling hand through my hair. It's still a little damp. Rhyson and I shower together most mornings. Have sex in the shower most mornings. Had sex this morning. I press my eyes shut and swallow back tears. How could I have been so careless?

"Could there be a mistake?" I ask desperately. "I mean, maybe there's been a mistake. I feel great. No symptoms whatsoever."

"Your urine test shows hCG levels." Dr. Allister shakes her head. "That's the hormone we're looking for when a woman is pregnant."

"But I . . . you're sure?"

"Yes, we're sure." A smile softens Dr. Allister's expression. "I'd like to do a transvaginal sonogram. That might make you more . . . certain."

"Like an ultrasound?"

"A little different. Not the jelly on the belly thing." Dr. Allister stands. "Slightly more intrusive, but it will help us determine how far along you are."

As soon as she says "how far along you are," I have visions of people walking up to me in grocery stores and in Starbucks, touching my swollen belly and asking when I'm due. This can't be happening.

"I'll get a technician in here to get it going."

Things are moving at warp speed, but I slow down long enough to think, to remember that Rhyson is in the waiting room. He has literally been having dreams about our unborn daughter for months. He should be here. Despite the dreams, neither of us imagined it would happen this quickly. We just got engaged last week.

"I need to call my fiancé." I grab my phone, take a deep breath and dial Rhyson.

"You ready?" he asks after not even a full ring. "That was quick."

"Um, yeah." I chew at the corner of my lip. "Could you come back here to examination room 4C?"

In the silence, his immediate concern reaches through the phone and wraps around me.

"Is something . . ." He clears his throat. "Are you okay, Pep?"

"I'm fine." I brighten the words to dispel his worry. "Could you just come back?"

It seems that I've barely hung up when the door swings open and Rhyson pokes his head in. I motion for him to step all the way into the room. He crosses the small space, butting his knees right up against mine and taking my hands in his.

"What's going on?" Concern darkens his silvery eyes to slate. "You okay?"

"Yeah, I just . . ." My glance drops to my hands linked with his in my lap. "The doctor just told me . . . I'm . . . I got a new phone."

He blinks at me several times before sputtering.

"What the—what the hell, Pep? You called me into the lady doctor's office to tell me you got a new damn phone?"

"Lady doctor?" An ill-timed giggle pops out of my mouth. "I haven't heard . . . I guess she is a lady doctor."

"Pep, for God's sake. What is it?"

"I got a new phone."

"Not this shit again." He tips his head back and heaves a long-suffering sigh.

"Let me tell you this my way."

"Your way is agonizingly slow. Meanwhile, I'm picturing a tumor the size of a watermelon on your ovaries. Spit it out."

"Because of the phone thing I missed my emails and voice mails," I rush on to say before he can interrupt again. "And I missed my appointment."

"Okay. You told me that." He squints at me, confusion all over his face. "That's why we're here, right?"

"I missed my shot, Rhyson," I say meaningfully. "You know. My birth control shot. By almost six weeks actually."

"Six weeks." I can see the facts connecting in his head before his eyes meet mine. A question is already forming there, but he doesn't ask the real question.

"So we've been having unprotected sex for six weeks. Is that what you're telling me?"

I nod, licking my lips and fidgeting with the edges of my paper gown.

"I'm pregnant," I whisper, afraid to raise my eyes. In case he's angry. In case he's as thrown as I am.

An almost undetectable sound from the air conditioner fan is all I hear for a few moments. When I finally look up, Rhyson's mouth is hanging open and his eyes are fixed on my stomach.

"You're . . . you're . . . what?" He sounds almost breathless.

"I'm preg—"

The rest of the word doesn't make it past my lips. Rhyson snatches me off the table and holds me so tight that if I had stuffing it would all be squeezed out of me. My feet dangle inches above the floor.

"Rhyson, baby, put me down," I mumble into his neck.

He sets me on my feet and pulls back to peer into my face. There is no anger or disappointment or uncertainty.

"This is amazing." He shakes his head, a dazed look still in his eyes. "I can't believe this. Oh, my God, Pep. Can you believe it?"

No, I really can't, but Dr. Allister's light tap on the door comes before I can respond.

"Okay to come in?" she asks. Her eyes flick to Rhyson, widening a little with recognition. "Mr. Gray, hello."

"Hi." Rhyson studies the cart the nurse rolls in behind the doctor. "I hear we're having a baby."

"I believe you are." She extends her hand. "Dr. Allister, by the way."

"Nice to meet you." He returns the handshake and offers that famous devastating smile. "Rhyson."

"Yes, well." Dr. Allister flushes a little while she snaps on rubber gloves. Always a comforting sound. "Let's take a look."

I smile weakly and lie back on the table when she instructs me to.

"I'm going to do a transvaginal ultrasound. It's the most accurate way to determine how far along you are," Dr. Allister says. "Are you fine with your fiancé being present for that?"

Rhyson looks slightly panicked like I might actually ask him to step outside and he'll miss something.

"I wouldn't have it any other way." I find his hand and squeeze.

Rhyson smiles, shifting his eyes from me to the doctor and then to the machine with the flat screen mounted on it.

I lie back and rest my feet in the stirrups. This should be incredibly awkward with Rhyson in the room, but he's near my head, holding my hand. His eyes never leave the screen even though there's nothing to see yet.

"You'll feel a different kind of pressure than with a typical pelvic exam," Dr. Allister says. "This probe will be moving around to get shots of what's going on inside."

The probe is a bit uncomfortable, but not too bad. It just takes a few seconds to get used to. A grey mass appears onscreen.

"Here's what we're looking for." Dr. Allister points to a dark blob in the grey sea of my uterus. "This is the gestational sac. The yolk sac that tells us for sure we've got a baby in there. About four weeks and a few days, I'd say."

I glance from the blobby uterine world onscreen to Rhyson's face. His expression is absolutely rapt, his attention fully taken by the little pouch our kid is living in.

"Is there a heartbeat?" Anxiety tightens his expression. "Shouldn't we hear a heartbeat?"

"Too early for that." Dr. Allister types in a few notes. "Next appointment maybe."

Rhyson releases my hand he's been clutching this whole time to aim his phone at the screen and presses record.

"We'll give you a 3D picture, Mr. Gray," Dr. Allister assures him.

"I just want my own." He shakes his head dazedly again. "This is just . . . wow."

Absolute awe and joy light up his expression. My emotions

aren't as straightforward. I do feel this incredible sense of connection with what looks like an ink blot in my uterus, but other emotions press in too. Fear. Disappointment. Maybe a little resentment. And, yes, guilt for even feeling anything less than the joy all over Rhyson's face. There are women who have been trying to get pregnant for years. And here I wasn't even trying, didn't even want it yet, and I'm . . .

Pregnant.

Once the machine is wheeled out, and Dr. Allister and Rhyson leave so I can get dressed, I'm left with just the little square print out of my ink blot. This little blob growing for the last few weeks inside of me just turned my life upside down, and I had no idea.

8

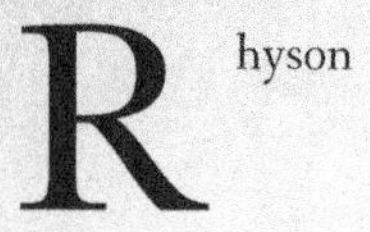

hyson

I CAN'T STOP WATCHING IT.

My phone glows in the unlit music room as I play the video over and over. I only recorded a few seconds of today's ultrasound. It's just this little smudgy sack in a grainy pool of Jell-O. There's not even any sound other than us breathing and Dr. Allister's voice. There's no heartbeat. No head or feet or fingers. No little peter.

Peter? I can't say dick now? I'm already censoring myself in my head. I guess peter is better than wiener or some other kid-appropriate name for cock. I'm already thinking like a father.

A father.

Shit. I'm gonna be a father. I am a father because I bet this child couldn't feel any more real to me if she were already here.

It's a girl, by the way.

All I've felt since Kai told me she was pregnant is joy, wonder, amazement. I can't even assign names to all the emotions that washed over me in that examination room. For the first time since today's appointment, fear and doubt creep in. What if I screw this kid up the way my parents screwed up on me? How much therapy would that take? Anything could happen. I Googled the first trimester, and Kai is more likely to miscarry over the next couple of months than at any other time during her pregnancy. Three minutes with that little blob, and I'd already do anything to protect it. To keep it. The same staunch protectiveness I feel for Kai instantly extended to our little blob.

"You okay?" Kai whispers from the doorway.

A wedge of darkness yields to the moonlight pouring in just beyond the wide windows, silhouetting her slim curves. The hem of my Jim Morrison t-shirt caresses her legs. She crosses one foot over the other, leaning her head against the doorframe.

"Why are we whispering?" I ask just as quietly, adding a smile that she slowly returns. "Come here."

I open my arms and wait for her to cover the few feet between the entrance and the piano where I'm seated. She settles on my knees, and I kiss her hair when she leans into me. I can't help it. One hand strays to her left ring finger, touching the glittering sign to the world that she belongs to me. My other hand covers her flat stomach holding our little secret. You can't see it, but my baby's in there, and it makes me feel a hundred feet tall.

"You couldn't sleep?" she asks.

"Too wired, I guess. Thinking about the baby." I scan her expression for any signs of the same excitement that has me out of bed at two o'clock in the morning. She's pulled that blank mask over her feelings. I'm not having it. I'll spend the rest of my life digging around in that pretty head and excavating her heart. I don't want to leave anything unspoken between us. Not ever again. We've been there and done that, and I want to give her everything. I'm only asking her for one thing in return.

Everything.

"If I ask you a question, will you be honest with me?" I tuck silky strands of dark hair behind her ear.

"Of course." In the faint glow of moonlight, she lowers her lashes before looking back up at me, waiting.

I cup her chin and brush my thumb over the lushness of her mouth.

"Do you want this baby?"

I've surprised her. Her eyes widen and then drop.

"I want this baby, yes." I will her to lift her eyes back to me and she eventually does. "In about three years."

I asked for that. We always say we want honesty until the truth slips in like a dagger between our ribs. I draw a sharp breath like she stabbed me.

"What are you saying? You want . . ." I can't even string the ugly words together. I can't even imagine that word anywhere near my baby.

"No!" Shock flashes across her face. She cups my face with both hands. "Oh, Rhys, no. I wouldn't. This is our baby. It never even crossed my mind. I promise."

I knew that. I know that. I believe her, but for just a second . . . relief steals over me, loosening the coiled muscles in my shoulders and neck.

"That came out wrong." She shakes her head and looks up at me, eyes earnest. "Really wrong. What I meant was I didn't want this now."

She traces a line from my neck and over my chest before blowing out a short breath.

"It's like I don't want this to happen now, but I do want our baby." She scrunches up her face. "I know how that sounds, but I'm trying to be honest with myself and with you."

"I know." I catch her hand and link it with mine to rest on my chest. "Keep talking. It's okay."

All she has is moonlight to see my face, but she scans my eyes and expression until something satisfies her that I mean it. That she doesn't have to hide from me.

"You know that my whole life, especially the last five years or so, felt like this series of stops and starts. Like as soon as I have any momentum, something blocks it. Something delays it."

Her fingers tighten around mine, squeezing to emphasize her next words.

"I was on birth control for a reason," she says. "I didn't want to have a baby right now. I'm coming off Luke's tour, finally with Prodigy, featured on one of the biggest albums of the year with Grip's song that's about to drop. And I was up next. We were launching my solo career next."

"And we still can, Pep." I stroke my knuckles over her cheekbone. "We still will."

Later.

I don't say the word out loud, but it somehow clangs as loud as a cymbal between us. She hears it. She knows it. It's the truth.

"Look." I tip my head back to consider the ceiling for a second before looking back to her, trying to match the unflinching honesty she offered me. "There's a lot we can do before the baby comes. We'll find the best producers for you to work with. Start getting songs together. And we can record throughout your pregnancy. You can be in the studio the whole time."

"But . . ." Kai plucks the unspoken word right out of my head. She waits for me to say what we both know I have to say.

"But I don't think we'll have the songs recorded and the videos done before you start showing," I continue. "And with dance being such a huge part of your brand, we'll need you in the best shape of your life for those, and for the tour. You got a taste of how grueling world tours are, but that was just opening for Luke. This would be your own show, with multiple sets. A different city every night. And I feel strongly that we'll get the most momentum if your world tour launches not too long after the album release."

"And since I can't do the world tour until after the baby is born, you'd want to wait on the album release." Her eyes find mine in the dim light. "Right?"

Right.

We stare at one another, each of us weighing our words. Waiting for the other to speak. She finally does.

"Are you telling me this as my baby daddy," she asks with a touch of lightness, even though her eyes offer no levity. "Or as my boss?"

"Does it matter?"

"Yeah, because if you're saying this as the father of my child, then you've been heard, and I'll take your opinion into account." She folds her bottom lip into her mouth. "If you're saying this as the head of my record label, then I don't have much choice, do I?"

There's no right answer. It's in this moment that I realize just how much therapy must have helped me. Love is not control. I don't want to control, Kai. I'm in a position of power over her, and I don't want it. I love her so much, I hate being the one holding the power to take away what she wants.

"So baby daddy or boss?" she whispers.

I thought there was no right answer, but when I look in her eyes, I see there's no wrong one either. Unconditional love bounces back at me. No matter what I say, we're together. We're getting married. We've having a baby. We'll launch her career. Everything will happen when it's supposed to as long as it's us.

"Both."

Regret and resignation wrestle in her eyes before she nods and kisses my lips lightly.

"Kai, there's so much we can do."

"But I was ready to do everything." She presses her lips against emotion. "To finally do it all now. And then in two years, three years, sure, we'd start a family."

"Time will fly,"

"That's much easier for you to say than it is for me to do." She closes her eyes and swipes at the lone tear escaping over her cheek. "I don't know if you can understand this, but all these emotions are warring inside me. I don't feel one more or less than the other."

She swallows and strokes her thumb over my hand still linked with hers.

"This baby, our baby," she leans forward until her lips float over mine, her breath cool on my lips, "Your baby inside me is the greatest joy I've ever had."

"You mean that?" My free hand winds into the hair tumbling past her shoulders, spearing into the heavy mass at her nape.

"Yes, I mean it." She sighs and reaches up to grip my wrist. "But at the same time, I'm so disappointed. You have to give me the space to be disappointed, Rhyson. To regret another missed opportunity, another delay."

I nod because I can do that.

"Don't ask me not to be ambitious," she adds earnestly. "Not to want to perform and to be the best artist I can be. Don't ask me to not want that."

"Kai, that's all part of what makes you the woman I'm crazy about." I press her a little closer. "Remember what we said? That we want to be known?"

I wait for her to nod, to recall the promises we made on the other side of our mistakes a few months ago. We hurt each other out of insecurity and mistrust, but we vowed to live our lives truly known, if by no one else in the world then by each other.

"I know you," I whisper, holding her eyes and wishing for more light so the shadows can't hide anything from me. "I see you, baby. I live you."

She grins at our own way of expressing that.

"I live you too." Her eyes seek mine to find the answering emotion that has to be there on my face because it's too massive to remain trapped inside of me. It must be spilling into my expression like a silent confession. "So with all that said, for the record, I am excited and amazed that we did this, that we made this baby together.

I saw our little blob today, and I just . . . I just already love . . . her or him."

"It's her." I slide our hands from my chest to rest between us and press into her stomach. "That's our little girl."

"You can't know for sure, Rhys, and I don't want you disappointed if it's a boy."

"I wouldn't be disappointed, and we'll know soon."

"You wanna find out?" she asks shyly.

"Hell, yeah, we're finding out." I scoff at even the notion of not finding out. "We need to know if we're planning for a boy or a girl. There's names. We have to get the name right. Nothing stupid or weird. Or Southern."

"Southern?" She laughs and sputters, all fake offended. "I don't even know what that means."

"Oh, you don't, Kai Anne?" I give her my "really" face accompanied by my best imitation of her Southern drawl.

"I thought you loved my name." She can't even hold the laugh back long enough to look affronted.

"Of course I do." I kiss her nose. "I just think we can do better."

I wince when she pinches me.

"Ow!" I snatch her closer and start tickling. She almost flips us both off the piano bench squirming and straining away from my fingers. The more I touch her, the less it's funny. The less we laugh. I go from searching out the spots that will make her squeal, to searching out her lips. She wraps her arms around my neck and dusts kisses across my cheeks, my nose, my chin. Affection gathers inside me until it brims over. She's my best friend. My whole world spins on this girl. She's my axis. I'm not sure how it happened, but she's the most essential thing in my life, and I'm humbled that she chooses to spend the rest of her life with me. Floored that she's having my baby.

She finds my hand, linking our fingers and bringing them up between us. "If I ask you a question, will you be honest with me?"

I asked her that earlier, and she answered with fearless honesty.

It's not as easy as it looks when you're staring down the barrel of that question.

"Yeah." I nod and run my palm over her silky hair. "Of course."

"What's going on with your hand?" She squeezes my right hand for emphasis.

Shit. She would ask me about the one thing I really don't want to talk about.

"Kai—"

"Tell me."

I slump against the piano, impervious to the discomfort of the keys digging into my back. I spread one hand over her hip to anchor her to my lap, or maybe to anchor myself.

"It's not quite right."

She doesn't respond right away. When I glance up at her face, I see all the reasons I didn't want to tell her. The guilt and devastation. I know she'll blame herself for this, and I don't want her to do that. Did it feel great slamming my fist into a brick patio? No, but I would do it again and again if it meant protecting her from scum like Malcolm and Drex. I'd cut it off if I had to.

"And that's why you gave Bristol such a hard time about playing next week in Vegas."

"Pep, it's not—"

"How not quite right?" Her eyes land on our hands linked together.

I pull my right hand from hers to curl and uncurl a fist.

"Maybe some loss of dexterity and control, which is huge for the way I play. Maybe the casual listener wouldn't hear it, but I do."

"Would I?"

I can't help but think about how I "hear" our love. The same way I "see" music in colors with my synesthesia, I hear our love like a song. The connection between us hums like a melody through my blood. I've never felt so in tune with another person, like there's a frequency we discovered in the wild for just the two of us.

"Would I, Rhys?" she asks again when I don't answer right away. "Would I hear the difference?"

"Probably." I hope she'll drop it, even though I know that's futile.

"Let me hear."

Shit.

"Pep, it's late." I rise up a few inches from the bench with Kai still cradled against me. "I have to be up and in the studio all day tomorrow."

She wiggles out of my arms and plants herself on the bench at the piano.

"Rhys, play." Her hand encircles my wrist, and she tugs me down beside her. "Please."

My hands are poised over the keys, but I hesitate. Music has been the one thing that made me exceptional. This instrument is what made me exceptional. I play many instruments, but the piano is where it all began. Where I've always shone brightest. The scariest thing in my world is mediocrity.

"What should I play?" I finally ask, sliding my eyes to the curves and lines of her profile.

"Play something I've heard before to see if I hear . . . the difference." Her eyes search mine in the barely lit inches separating us. "Play my song."

Despite the heaviness of my heart and the soreness of my hand, a gravelly chuckle scrapes in my throat.

"Which one? They're all yours lately."

She laughs and lowers her lashes like the truth makes her shy. Nothing inspires me more than Kai. Every song on my next album somehow ties to her, to our life together. To our past. To our future.

"'My Soul to Keep.'" She drops her rumpled head to my shoulder.

"I'll play if you sing it with me."

She tenses beside me, telegraphing her typical reluctance to sing in front of me before she nods against my shoulder.

From the first notes, I hear the deficit. When I was young, I didn't truly appreciate my gift. It came so easily at first I thought it was magic until I started instruction, started polishing a gift that was very much in the rough. And after all those years, all that was dazzling, at least to my ears, feels reduced to a mere glimmer. I didn't realize how completely this defined me until it was threatened.

No one but me has heard the difference. My fingers falter because I can't stand for anyone to hear, to know that I may have lost something I foolishly took for granted. The ease of perfection. I don't want Kai to hear. As soon as I stop, she presses my fingers back to the keys, narrowing her eyes at me.

"You said you'd play if I sang with you." She lifts one dark brow. "We're just coming to the first verse. Why'd you stop?"

"Do you hear the difference?" I ask softly, shifting my eyes to my hands hovering over the keys. My right hand looks the same, but something hasn't healed that the doctors assured me should have by now.

"Maybe." She shrugs. "You've barely played anything. Are we gonna sing or what?"

"Pep." I drop my hands to my lap.

"Rhyson." She covers them with hers, leaning forward and around so I'm forced to look at her. "You said you wanted to be known, but you won't even play a song you wrote for me? What if it were me? What if I was the one keeping something this important from you?"

She's right. I remember what that felt like. When I discovered she'd cut me out of the sex tape fiasco, I felt betrayed. Yes, because she lied, but also because she didn't trust me to be able to handle anything and not walk away.

Without acknowledging that she's made her point, I start from the top with the few measures of instrumentation before the words come in. I begin, and she joins in.

I was lost before you found me, or maybe I found you
Maybe it was fate or kismet, or something much more true

It could have been an answered prayer, a sacred certainty
All I know is what we have now. I've got no plans to leave
Not an ocean, not forever
Nothing wide or deep
Will ever end this love between us
My soul is yours to keep

The arrangement requires her voice to vault from sweet, husky alto to a soprano that soars, all the while weaving in and out, our voices dancing then sparring. Her harmony, companion to my anchoring melody. An unquiet silence follows the final note. Though I'm done playing, though we've stopped singing, the sounds left an impression in the air around us. My ears won't let go, clinging to the memory of our voices together. I wonder if Kai still hears it too.

"So . . ." I clear my throat. "Did you notice any difference?"

"Yes, I was much more relaxed than the last time we sang together," she says with a straight face. "I'm getting better."

"Pep, come on." Her words coax a grin out of me even as I wait for the verdict.

"It's not that bad, Rhys."

"Not that bad?" I gape at her. "I was 'not that bad' when I was three years old. Is anything as mediocre as 'not that bad'?"

I shove my fingers into my hair. Damn. It's even worse than I thought.

"You didn't let me finish, prima donna." She traps my hands between hers. "You sound magnificent like you always do, but I know what you mean. I hear what you're saying. It's subtle, but I spent too many nights on my bed in Glory Falls listening to your album not to detect even the smallest change."

"So you do hear it?" I knew I wasn't imagining it, but to hear her say it sinks my heart a little more.

"Like I said, it's subtle. I don't think most people would notice. And it probably is just dexterity. Hopefully something more therapy can address. Maybe see the doctor before we leave for Vegas?"

"Can't." I shake my head and lace our fingers together. "He's in Poland for the next two weeks."

"Who goes to Poland?" Kai grimaces, I have to laugh at her expression.

"I hear Poland's a perfectly beautiful place."

"I've never been. You can take me some day." She allows a bit of a smile on her lips. "We'll go see him when he gets back from Poland."

"We?" I tilt my head down to search her eyes.

"Yes, we. I honestly think it's something that can easily be fixed." Kai climbs onto my lap to rest her forehead against mine and hang her arms over my shoulders. "But I'm still trying not to feel guilty about this, Rhys."

"Baby, no." She's so petite my two hands almost span her entire back. "Don't do that. Don't think that. That's exactly why I didn't tell you."

"I know, but . . ." She swallows and squeezes her eyes closed. "If I hadn't . . . God, that one night has caused us so many problems."

That one night with Drex has caused us a lot of problems—a lot of pain—but I don't care as long as I get to spend the rest of my life with this girl. She's worth anything.

"So can I come with you to the doctor?" Her breath whispers over my lips.

"Yeah. You know why?" I smile against her mouth. "Because everything is easier with you."

"Easy?" She teases me with her eyes, slipping her hand between us to wrap around my ever-hardening dick. "This doesn't feel easy. It feels pretty hard to me."

She grinds into me, a slow, deep move that marries her heat to my hardness. I stifle a groan, and my cock strains against my sleep pants. I was really trying to be good tonight. My hands smooth down her back, edge into her panties to stroke over her ass.

"What'd Dr. Allister say about . . ." I open my mouth over the silkiness of her throat, tonguing the hollow at the base.

"About what?" Her words melt into a moan as I twist a nipple between my fingers. I slide my mouth up to her ear, sucking on her earlobe.

"About fucking," I drop the word in her ear, absorbing the shudder of her body against me. I bend to bite her nipple through her shirt.

"We're good," she gasps. "We're fine. I mean, we can."

Her hands plunge into my pants, and she drags her finger deep between the cheeks of my ass.

It should not feel that good, but damn it really does.

"Let me eat your pussy," I whisper to her hotly, my mouth watering.

"Let me suck your dick," she whispers back, her eyes teasing and taunting and promising.

"Okay." I slump my back against the piano and let her go. "You twisted my arm."

She slides off the bench and between my knees. I lift my hips just enough for her to shimmy the pants down over my thighs and around my ankles. Her mouth is like a wet furnace around me, scorching the sensitive head. She sips at the drops leaking from the tip. Her moans reverberate around my cock as her hands work my balls. There's no finesse. No technique. No checking to see if she's pleasing me. Just her own raw hunger. I recognize it because that's what I feel every time I taste her. She's back and forth. Up and down. Feasting on me, lips stung and red, stretched around me. Eyes closed tightly and brows pinched together like she can't suck it hard enough, fast enough. Her eyes open and peer up at me like a little cat lapping the cream.

Did I say I had power over her?

She has all of it and she knows it. Her hands splay over my thighs, pushing and spreading me wider as she sinks deeper, her head bobbing slow and then fast. Setting her own pace, she exercises supremacy over me as I dissolve from the inside. Fisting her hair, I send my cock deeper until the tip slips into the tight black hole of her throat. I can tell it's almost too much. A tear slides from the corner of her eye, and a mixture of the juices from her mouth and my dick saturates the corners of her lips. It's the most erotic thing I've ever seen. My balls tighten in warning.

"Babe," I gasp and pull out. "I don't want to come in your mouth."

"Whatever you want." Her eyes, wide and willing, tell me she means it. "You know that."

I've been storing this fantasy in the back of my head ever since I heard she's pregnant. Thinking about the first time I'm inside her knowing she's carrying my baby. I slide to the floor beside her, pressing her back into the thick pile rug. I slowly ease up the t-shirt, revealing first a pair of the panties I bought her. I trace the wet spot her pussy leaked through the shell pink silk.

"Sucking me off turns you on?"

I know it does. She's told me it does, but I love seeing the evidence for myself. She just nods and opens her legs wider like the gate to a city eager to be conquered. She has these subtle ways of directing me. I rub circles over the sensitive skin inside her thighs, and then suckle the soft spots behind her knees. She is my delicacy. My sweet, fragile treat. By the time I reach the little pink panties, she's twisting and writhing. I lay my lips against the wet circle left by her arousal and nudge her panties aside with my nose. I draw in the sweet muskiness of her scent.

"God, Pep," I groan. "Even your smell is addictive."

"Rhyson, baby." A subtle roll of her hips brushes my lips against her wetness. "Please."

I ease up past the waistband of her panties and have to stop at her stomach. I kiss the taut skin of her waist reverently, dipping my tongue into the shallow well of her bellybutton. I flick a glance up to find her eyes soft on me.

"We're having a baby," she whispers, working her fingers into my hair.

I know she's disappointed that we'll have to adjust her debut release schedule. I have no doubt she's conflicted about it, but right now, all I see is joy reflected back to me.

"Thank you, Kai." My voice is husky with passion and gratitude.

"If you really want to thank me . . ." Mischief and desire shade her dark eyes.

I grin and knead one breast under the t-shirt while slipping two fingers inside of her. Oh, my God. She's soaking wet and tight. With my whole hand, I massage the juices all over her pussy and then trail my finger down to the puckered entrance between her cheeks. She goes completely still. I do it again, rubbing her wetness over that tightly rimmed mystery.

"Has anyone ever had this, Pep?" If she says yes I'll probably lose my shit.

"No," she whispers, her eyes holding mine in the moonlight.

I press my thumb against this last frontier.

"When can I have it?"

She gulps, but her eyes never leave me.

"I'm yours. You know that."

That is so the right damn answer. Not tonight, though. The first time we do that, I'll take my time making sure she's ready. If I want her to do anal more than once, I better get it right the first time. And I already know if I get in there, once won't be enough.

My thumb shifts back to her clit, circling and pressing and pinching, all the while rolling and kneading her breast. Her eyelids fall. She slaps a palm over her forehead and bites her lip, trapping a moan in her mouth. Her orgasm quakes through her, and her thighs tremble. I want that. To feel her shaking and tightening around me. I press her knees back as far as they can go until she's wide open, the thick pink lips a tempting exhibition between her legs.

"You're sure this is okay?" Even though the doctor said it was fine, I find myself worrying about the baby because I already know how hard I'm going to fuck her. "I can try to be gentle."

"You better not be."

Her breathy answer snaps my control. I anchor her heels around my waist and push inside. She's so small, so tight, but she takes it all every time. The only thing better than that first thrust is the second and then the third. And, oh God, that fourth one. I pull her legs over my shoulders and insinuate myself deeper. Her body obliges every swollen inch of me. I'm fucking her like an animal in blind heat. We moan in unison, surrendering to the erotic toil of our bodies.

"Pep, this is . . ." The words get lost in the hurricane churning between us.

"Yeah, it is." She arches her back off the floor, and her eyes roll back. "Baby, I'm coming again."

I peel the t-shirt over her head, catching the sleeves at her elbows and trapping her arms over her head. Her breasts, small and perfect with those raspberry nipples, the subtly muscled stomach, the elegant rib cage bearing the scripted prayer. My eyes drop to where we're joined. I watch myself come out just a little, coated with her juices. Seeing that triggers some atavism in me, some ancient instinct to claim. I thought this first time with the baby would be poignant, but there's a savage edge to it. My eyes flicker from the golden canvas of her body to her eyes. She knows me so well.

"Whatever you want, Rhyson," she encourages. "You can have. You can do."

That unquestioning acquiescence is all it takes. I jerk out of her body and roll my hand up and down my dick, almost collapsing from how good it feels. I spend every ounce, spraying her stomach and breasts. Patterning her torso with my love and possession. I run my fingers through the thick, warm cream, working it into her skin. I check her face to see if I've totally grossed her out, but her cheeks go a deeper pink. Her breath comes faster, bouncing her breasts with the furious in and out of air. Her eyes drop to my cock in my hand, and she licks her lips, again signaling what she wants from me.

I lean up until I'm right over her mouth and rub the tip of my cock over her lips, painting them wet and shiny. Her little pink tongue darts out to swipe across her lips to taste me. I don't care that she is wet and sticky with my cum. I throw myself down on the rug beside her and pull her into my chest and tuck her head under my neck.

"Too rough?" I ask quietly into her wild hair.

"Hmmmmmm." Her tongue darts out to lick across my neck and shoulder. "What do you think?"

I kiss her hair and roll my palm over one strong, smooth leg.

"You love me?"

"I adore you." She rests her head on my chest, her eyelids drooping over her sated gaze. "You know that."

"Good. Because you're stuck with me for life."

"For life isn't long enough." She snuggles closer, her voice fading with sleep. "Promise me forever."

9

Rhyson

I CAN'T BELIEVE I'VE BEEN IN the studio all day. I squeeze the bridge of my nose and roll my shoulders. Marlon's project is almost done. Just these last few songs. The engineers are waiting to master the files, but I can't stop tinkering with the mix on this Otis Redding sample. Well, that's the one I've been working on the last hour or so. Before that it was track number four. Before that it was track number eight. I can't remember which track was before that, but I know my obsessive perfectionism has confined me to this one room for hours.

"Still at it?" Amber, the closest thing to a receptionist Wood has, sets my favorite energy drink down beside me. "You know what time it is?"

I pop open the can, guzzle a few swallows, and grab my phone to check the time.

Eight o'clock. Gep was supposed to drop Kai off thirty minutes ago after some photo shoot Bristol set up. Sometimes my reception back here sucks, and my phone doesn't even ring.

"Did Gep call up front?" I scroll through my missed calls and check my text messages. Nothing.

"No." Amber offers me a slip of paper. "This guy did call while you were in here. He claimed to be Kai's father."

My eyes move from the phone to Amber's face.

"James Pearson?" I ask.

She glances at the paper before offering it to me again.

"Yep." Her next words trip over each other in her haste. "You said to only bother you if it was Kai or an emergency, and I wasn't even sure the guy was legit. Should I have?"

"Nah, you're good." What the hell does he want?

"Cool." She gathers her tawny colored locs off her neck and into a ponytail. "Well, he left his number and asked you to call him."

"Okay." I rub the paper between my fingers for a second and look back up at her. "But nothing from Gep or Kai?"

"Nope. Sorry." She shifts her backpack with one arm. "You need anything before I head out?"

I shake my head absently while I dial the number on the paper she gave me.

"Nah. G'night." I flick my chin up at her while the phone rings on the other line.

"Hello," a deep voice answers with just a hint of a Southern accent.

"Uh, Mr. Pearson?"

"Yes." He seems to hesitate. "Is this Rhyson?"

"Yeah." I lean back and prop my feet on the studio console. The guys would kill me, but just this once. "I got a message you called me here at the studio earlier."

"Yes. I didn't have your personal number obviously, but heard you owned this studio." He releases a heavy breath over the line. "I wasn't sure how to handle things, so I just thought I'd try by starting with you."

"Handle what things?"

I keep my voice neutral even though I don't like this man. He hurt Kai more than anyone has, except maybe me. I imagine my Kai sitting on a broken step as a little girl, wearing her tutu and ballet slippers, waiting for a father who never came home.

No, I don't like this man at all.

"Cassie, that's my daughter . . . my other daughter's name," he says. "She saw on one of those entertainment shows that you and Kai Anne got engaged."

I don't respond, but wait for him to reach his point.

"Well, I, uh . . ." Discomfort weights his words. "Congratulations."

"Thank you." Still waiting for the point of this call.

"I'd like to be . . . well, involved somehow seeing as how I'm Kai's father."

Oh, now he remembers that he's her father.

"You'll need to talk to Kai about that," I answer stiffly.

"Well, she's not much for talking to me these days." He offers a rough, rueful chuckle. "I thought maybe you could . . ."

His words fade into a pained silence that I don't try to make any easier for him.

"I used to wonder how I'd feel on her wedding day, ya know?" he continues, regret smudging his words. "When she was a little girl, I couldn't imagine giving her away to someone else."

"No one gives Kai to me. She's already mine."

It just comes out because . . . well, because it's true. I probably could have handled that better, said it more tactfully, but the thought of this man, absent for so long from Kai's life, presuming to have any rights on what will be our day, agitates me. Tension clogs the silence between our two lines for a moment before he responds.

"A little possessive there, aren't ya?" he half-laughs.

I'm too tired for this, and don't bother holding back a long exhale of breath.

"Mr. Pearson, what do you want from me?"

"I know it's Kai's decision if I'm invited—"

"Yeah, it is," I agree. "I wouldn't blame her if she doesn't involve you. I'm not sure she should."

"You are marrying my daughter, you know," he says softly, but not soft enough to disguise that he's offended.

"Mr. Pearson, if Kai's mother were alive, I would have asked for her blessing." My voice trades weariness for irritation. "But she isn't, so I flew to Glory Falls to ask Aunt Ruthie for her blessing. Then I flew her to LA so she could witness me propose to the girl she's practically raised since you deserted Kai and her mother. You have no rights in this situation, and I'd appreciate it if you'd stop acting like you've been around for the last fifteen years. It's making me sick and it's making me angry."

A startled silence follows my words. I draw a deep breath, suppressing the ire that rises the longer I talk to him.

"Rhyson, I can tell you love my daughter very much."

He pauses as if waiting for me to affirm. I don't, but just wait for him to finish.

"I had some hard choices to make back then, and I didn't always make the right ones, but I'm living with the consequences. I'm trying to make things right."

"The day I marry Kai will be the happiest of my life," I say quietly. "I don't want awkwardness. I don't want old hurts making things less than perfect. To be frank, I'm not even sure I'll invite my own mother. If Kai decides she's ready for you to be involved in her life that way, I'll support her. If she decides she's not, I'll support her. I just want her happy."

"That's what I want, too." His sigh from the other end is resigned. "Cassie says she and Kai are meeting when you come to Vegas next week."

"Yeah. I think my sister has tickets to the showcase for her. For you both actually." I glance at my watch, remembering that Kai and Gep are late. "Look, I need to go. Like I said, you'll need to talk to Kai about all this."

"I understand." The sadness in his voice tweaks my sympathy. "Well, maybe I'll see you next week in Vegas."

"Maybe," I reply noncommittally.

"Thank you for taking care of her," he says before ending the call.

I hold the phone for a few seconds. I don't want to feel sorry for the guy at all, but I do. Kai refused to see me for three months, and it was the most miserable three months of my life. Not the same, but I do empathize.

"Hey, handsome."

I look up to find Kai standing at the door, a grin on her face.

I motion her in, grabbing her around the waist when she's close enough and sitting her on my lap.

"You're late." I bury my face in the curve of her neck and shoulder, silky tendrils of hair tickling my nose. She looks casual from the neck down in her jeans and tank top. Her hair is pulled up into a messy bun of some sort, with little wisps escaping and making her adorable. Her face, though, is still fully made up from the photo shoot.

"I'm sorry." She trails kisses over my chin and down my neck. "The shoot went over."

"What's it for again?"

"People Magazine's breakout stars, or something like that. I'll have to ask Bristol to be sure."

"I was just about to call Gep." I pull her a little closer and inhale the scent of pears and cinnamon lingering on her skin.

"I could drive myself to these things, you know."

"Sure, but you need security with you anyway, so he may as well, right?"

Her mouth cements into an obstinate line. We've had this argument more than once. I push. She pulls. She doesn't think she needs security. I insist. Her lips part, and I already see the protest on her face before it has a chance to leave her mouth.

"I just got off the phone with your dad." I figure this will distract her from an argument for now.

"My dad?" Surprise colors her expression. "He called you?"

"Yeah. Well, he called the studio and left his number so I could call him."

"What did he want?"

"I think to be invited to our wedding." I rub the little soft wisps of hair between my fingers and watch her expression.

"He doesn't think he's gonna give me away, does he?" She draws back a little, irritation on her face.

"I told him no one gives to me what's already mine."

She giggles and palms one side of my face.

"You said that to my father?"

My hand cups her breast through the tank top and I rub my thumb roughly over the nipple until it beads. I nip at the silky, scented skin of her neck with my teeth.

"Is it not true?" I whisper, loving the constellation of goose bumps sprouting on her arms.

She nods and tips her head back, shifting on my lap.

"Wait till I get you home," I say against the fragile line of her collarbone. "I'll remind you how true it is."

"Why wait?" Her eyes toy with me. "I seem to remember putting a piano to good use here once before."

A husky chuckle crosses my lips.

"Too many people here tonight. We'd get caught."

"The risk kinda makes it more exciting though," she says, voice husky and eyes simmering. "Don't you think?"

"I'm not risking anyone seeing more of you than they should." I stand up, taking her with me and setting her on her feet. "So let's go home so I can make love to you."

"Will you take a bath with me?" She slips her hands under my t-shirt, her palms gliding over my back, provoking a shudder through me.

"Yes." I bend to kiss her hair. "You want me to fuck you in the tub again?"

"Yeah, if you're taking requests." She yawns and her lashes droop over drowsy eyes.

"Come on. Let's get you home. It's been a long day."

We're making our way across the dimly lit parking lot before it occurs to me she could be tired because of the baby.

"Did you pick up the prenatal vitamins Dr. Allister prescribed?"

"Man, I forgot." She looks up at me, her eyes sparking just a little. "I guess I'm this tired because of the baby. Kinda cool, huh?"

"Not cool." I bring her knuckles up to my lips. "We'll get them tomorrow."

When we reach my truck, she slumps against the passenger side door. My hands find her waist and settle low on the curve of her hips as I bend to steal one more kiss before we get on the road.

"Did it rain?" She glances over her shoulder.

"Not for a long time. That's why our grass looks the way it does, babe."

"No, something's wet." She arches away from the side of the car, reaching back to touch her shirt. She rubs her fingers together. "Ew! It's sticky."

I touch the side of the car to investigate the wetness and notice something hanging over the side. I grab the lump of soaked cotton.

"Fuck!" Even in the barely lit parking lot I can see that the t-shirt is soaked in something red that I suspect is blood. The passenger side door is covered with it.

"What is that?" Kai asks nervously, peering down at the t-shirt I haven't dropped yet.

An icy hand punches right through my chest.

It's one of those "Mrs. Rhyson Gray" t-shirts fans are always wearing, but it's drenched in blood and has slashes through it, as if from a knife. I toss it back onto the car, hoping I haven't disrupted any forensic evidence by touching it. I wipe my hands across my jeans and dig my phone out of my pocket. I pull Kai away from the car and practically drag her back towards the studio. My glance bounces all around the parking lot for any sign of danger or anyone ready to hurt her. The person who did this could still be close. Could be here right now. Could be watching us.

"Rhyson," Gep responds on the first ring. "Sorry about getting Kai there late. I should have texted."

"Forget that." Voice terse, I gently urge Kai into the safety of the studio. "We have bigger problems. I need you at Wood as soon as possible."

"Maybe it was just a sick joke." Kai looks at our stained hands. Now that we're in the bright lights of Wood's reception area, we can clearly see that it's blood.

"Well, I'm not laughing." My face is so grim it aches. "And when I find out who did this, they won't be either."

10

ai

"WE'RE NOT GOING TO VEGAS."

Rhyson's declaration swivels all heads in his direction. It's been a long night. We're finally home, and everyone's assembled around the kitchen table. I watch every face for reaction. Gep doesn't look surprised, but just nods. Disappointment, then resignation flashes over Grip's handsome face. Bristol doesn't bother hiding her outrage.

"The hell we aren't going to Vegas." She pops to her feet, hands already fisted on her hips. "It was an awful, stupid thing someone did tonight, but it's not going to stop us."

"Bristol, I'm not arguing about this with you." Rhyson faces away from us, arms stretched out to the side, hands gripping the counter tightly, muscles bunched under his t-shirt.

"Yeah, we will argue if you think that months of planning is going down the drain because some super fan poured pig's blood all over your car." Bristol plants her hands on her slim hips. "I know it's freaking you out, but—"

"Oh, you know?" Rhyson faces her, propping his back against the counter. "You know how it felt to see 'Die Bitch' written in blood on my window? To know that's meant for Kai? That someone out there could seriously want her dead?"

I train my eyes on the table, clutch my glass of water, and draw in deep, calming breaths. Once we got back inside the studio, Gep and the cops came. They saw the ominous message written on the passenger side window, in addition to the slashed, bloody t-shirt. I want to dismiss it as a silly prank, but it's too sinister. It doesn't feel like a joke. There's nothing funny about someone wanting you dead, much less writing it in blood.

I'm startled by Bristol's hand squeezing my shoulder. Her sympathetic eyes apologize for something that isn't her fault. She walks over to her brother and leans against the counter beside him to take his hand.

"I know it's a lot." When he tries to pull away, she won't let go. She dips her head, forcing him to meet her eyes. "It's scary, but Rhyson, we can't just cancel this trip."

"We can." He pulls away and walks over to the refrigerator to grab one of his energy drinks. "We will."

"No, we won't." Bristol firms her lips. "You do you realize this is being streamed online? Media outlets from all over the country, from all over the world, are sending reporters? We have interviews scheduled. Appearances. The showcase itself. A contract with the hotel, who's been billing this for months. All of you have fans flying in just for this."

When Bristol lays out the full scope of the showcase, it's apparent we can't just cancel Vegas. I see it on Grip and Gep's faces. Despite the fear coiled in my stomach, I know that. We're all just waiting for Rhyson to arrive at the same inevitable conclusion.

"Okay." He nods and joins us at the table. "You guys go. Kai and I will stay here."

"It doesn't work that way, Rhyson." Bristol massages her temples. "You are the linchpin. None of this works without you."

"Well, I'm not going anywhere without Kai." Rhyson glances at me briefly before looking away to the can he holds. "And I don't want her going. It's too much. Too many people. Too many variables we can't control."

"Gep, tell him we can keep Kai safe," Bristol urges.

Gep clears his throat before speaking.

"You know we can, Rhys," he says.

"No, Gep, I don't know that." A deep "v" settles between Rhyson's eyebrows. "If I knew that, we wouldn't be having this discussion now."

"Well, we can," Gep says. "We've always kept you safe. This isn't our first time dealing with a stalker."

That word "stalker" makes me tense up even more. If it were up to me, I'd lock me and Rhyson and this baby upstairs in our bedroom behind a bolted door. I know Rhyson is concerned about me, but I'm just as concerned about him.

"Kai, talk some sense into him." Bristol adds pleading eyes to her request.

"Don't do that, Bris," Rhyson says sharply. "Don't use her against me like that."

"I'm not using her against you." Bristol rubs a hand across the back of her neck. "Sometimes she's the only one you'll listen to."

Rhyson and I stare at each other across the table. As much as I don't want to go to Vegas either, we'll have to. It's not just us. It's the band and Luke and Grip. They all have a lot riding on this showcase.

"I keep thinking . . . wondering . . ." He looks away from me, dismissing the words he didn't speak with a quick shake of his head.

"What?" I ask. "You keep wondering what?"

"Well, I've always gone to such trouble to protect my privacy, and the one time I put it all out there, it's come back to haunt me."

"What do you mean?"

"Our engagement was everywhere. I proposed in front of fifty people, and videos of it went viral. If I hadn't—"

"Don't even think that." I lean over to cup his face, looking into his eyes. "I love the way you proposed to me. I love that we took our story back, that you wanted the whole world to know I'm your girl. Some sicko wishing it was her doesn't change that for me."

He pushes the hair over my shoulder, his fingers caressing my neck.

"For once I wanted everyone to know something about me," he says quietly. "The fact that you love me and choose to spend the rest of your life with me—there's nothing I'm prouder of. Nothing. I didn't want to hide it or disguise it or pretend I'm not happy with you."

"We are not going to live our lives like hostages." I blink back tears.

He nods and drops a kiss on my nose.

"Exactly," Bristol says, reminding me we aren't alone. "That's why we're going to Vegas."

Rhyson levels an exasperated look at his sister.

"You never let up, do you?"

"It's my job to not let up." Bristol shrugs.

"No one can ever accuse you of not doing your job," Grip mutters.

"And that's a bad thing?" Bristol locks, loads, and aims a look at Grip. "What do you think we should do? This is your career too."

"Whatever Rhyson decides," Grip says with a lift of his broad shoulders, "I'll accept. I'm good."

"I'm fighting on this for you." Bristol sighs and shakes her head. "For you and Luke and the guys who've been busting their asses at festivals for the last year."

"I know, Bris," Grip says softly. "And we appreciate it, but Rhys and I were boys before this label, and that ain't changing. I know this is important, but I'm a friend first."

"And I'm not a sister first?" She narrows her eyes at him. "Why do you think I bust my ass for him? For the money?"

"Nobody thinks that," Rhyson cuts in. "You know I appreciate all you do. Somebody has to be the bad guy, and you're usually it. You always do the shit no one else wants to do. You're always the adult in the room."

He stands to his feet, pulling me with him. He offers Bristol his first smile since the parking lot.

"I think you secretly want to run this label yourself." He laughs softly and hooks an elbow around her neck, drawing her head down to his shoulder so she's tucked under one arm and I'm under the other. "And you probably could. You think I don't know I wouldn't be where I am without you?"

Bristol turns into her brother's side.

"I know you're freaked." She looks up at him, her expression as resolved as her brother's. "But don't give this idiot that much power."

"This isn't a power struggle," Rhyson says. "I don't have anything to prove to this person or to myself. All I want is to keep Kai safe."

He glances down at me so our eyes meet and hold. I wish everyone would leave. We haven't had a moment alone since the parking lot. I want him to hold me, to calm the fear that I won't allow myself to express, even to him. But if I'm in his arms, it will fade. If we were alone, I'd climb into his lap and bury myself in him.

"Look, it's been a long night." Bristol grabs her ever-present bag of tricks, which could hold everything from her iPad to a cure for cancer, as far as I know. "Why don't we get out of your hair and let you and Kai get some rest?"

Should I add mind-reader to Bristol's varied talents? I send her a grateful glance, which she returns with a quick smile.

"We'll revisit this in the morning," she says. "Just call me as soon as you're up, k?

Rhyson nods while he and Grip dap each other up.

"Gep, you're staying here tonight, right?" A slight frown disrupts Rhyson's expression.

"Yeah." Gep stands up and stretches. "We've got several guys from the team staying, posted all over."

"Okay." Rhyson hesitates before going on. "Could we go over the adjustments you're making to the security plan just one more time?"

I could tell him the adjustments myself by now since Rhyson has asked this question twice already in the last few hours.

"Sure," Geps replies without complaint, sitting down at the table again.

"Hey." Rhyson presses his lips to my hair and turns me toward the rear staircase. "I'll be up in a little bit. Wait for me."

I tip up on my toes to kiss him, say goodnight to Gep, and head up the stairs to our bedroom. The tank top I'd worn, stained with blood, is long gone. I'd washed as much as I could at the studio and thrown on some random shirt from the storage closet, but I need a shower. Even having washed earlier, traces of blood still slip away from my body and down the drain. I follow the crimson trail with my eyes until it has completely disappeared.

I finally wash off the heavy makeup from the People Magazine shoot. God, that shoot seems like it was years ago. I was answering frivolous questions about how Rhyson proposed. Being coy about the wedding date and the location, none of which we've even talked about. I had no idea there was someone out there incensed by our engagement. I can only assume that's what triggered this craziness.

I stare back at my reflection. My face, scrubbed and shiny. Shadows color the skin under my eyes. I look tired. And scared.

Perfect love casts out fear.

I haven't thought of that verse in ages. There was a little song we used to sing in Vacation Bible School to memorize it. Daddy would remind me of that verse when I had nightmares or was scared of something. In one of his sermons, he said love and fear shouldn't occupy the same space. So many of the things I believe, that guide and comfort me, came from a man I don't trust. A man I don't even know anymore because he left and never looked back.

And yet . . .

I dig in the closet, rooting around through shoes and belts and dresses until I find what I'm looking for. Ella bought this t-shirt at one of Rhyson's concerts and gave it to me as a joke. In a tiny act of defiance, I slip it on, letting it settle over my shoulders. I close my eyes, waiting for the fear, but I look down at the simple lettering and only feel peace. Whoever was behind tonight's drama doesn't get to win. They aren't going to paralyze me. Perfect love does cast out fear, and if there is one thing Rhyson and I have, it's love.

When I walk back into the bedroom, he's seated on the edge of the bed staring off into space. I stand between his legs, waiting for his response to the shirt I'm wearing. He traces the lettering with a finger.

"Mrs. Rhyson Gray, huh?" He cracks a small smile, but his eyes remain sober.

"I will be very soon."

"I told you that you already are." He kisses my chin just above him. "What are we waiting for? Wanna go ahead and make it official?"

I draw back a few inches, crinkling my brow.

"It is official. We're engaged."

"Why wait?" He drops his eyes to his knees briefly before looking back to me. "Let's go ahead and get married."

My heart performs a triplet in my chest. I remind myself that he's either joking or traumatized, and that I should calm my tits.

"We will when the time is right." I rest my arms on his shoulders, searching his eyes. "That's not a decision we make after a night like we've had."

"It has nothing to do with what happened tonight. I don't want a long engagement, Pep."

"Okay. Then we won't have one." I kiss the corners of his mouth. "Let's talk about it later."

I press all my weight into him, trying to topple him back, but he doesn't budge. I settle for rolling onto the bed and pulling him down with me, facing away from him so that he's spooning me. He sifts strands of my hair through his fingers and buries his nose in the unruliness of it. We just lie in silence, as close as we've been to peaceful for hours. His arm wraps around my waist, fingers splayed over my stomach.

"So how are my two favorite girls?"

I can't help but laugh and press my back deeper into his chest.

"We've talked about this." I place my hand over his where it rests on my stomach. "It's too early to know."

"Oh, I know." He pushes my hair aside to kiss my neck. "I can't wait to hear her heartbeat and see her fingers. How do I love her so much already?"

"I know. I love her," I glance over my shoulder and grin, "Or him already too."

Perfect love casts out fear.

We're avoiding the thing we have to talk about. The thing that wrecked our night and twisted me into knots for the last few hours.

"Let's go to Vegas," I whisper, braced for all his arguments. Prepared for a tirade. He stiffens behind me, resting his head against mine for a few seconds before gently rolling me over to face him.

"I know what Bristol said, but don't let her—"

"It's not Bristol." I chuckle with little humor. "Though she does make a great point. It's a lot to renege on when we're just getting started."

"I don't give a fuck." His words and eyes are fierce. He lifts my chin so I have to look at him. "Not one fuck. You're all I care about. You and this baby."

"We'll be fine."

"Tonight was not some random joke. That person knew where the cameras were in the parking lot. They knew to conceal their face. They went to the trouble of getting animal blood from somewhere and doing this. They—"

"I know." I press a finger to his lips to stem the words. "Baby, I know."

"Look at me." He thrusts his fingers into my hair, angling my head up to meet the ferocity of his stare. "I will not lose you. Not over some stupid showcase in Vegas."

"So we shut down our lives until we figure out who did this?" I push his hair back and shake my head. "We don't have enough evidence. We may never know."

"So we just wait for them to do something even worse and hope they slip up? No. I'm not risking you."

His hollow laugh blows across my lips.

"You don't get it. None of you do." He closes his eyes and presses his forehead to mine. "There was a time when music and building this label meant everything to me. When all the things Bristol said down there would have persuaded me, but that's not the case anymore."

He looks at me, and the same fear that stared back at me in the mirror shadows his eyes.

"You think I'll give a damn about music or Prodigy or any of it if something happens to you?" He shakes his head, looking a little haunted. "I've dealt with stalkers before, Kai, and I know how quickly things can escalate. And no matter how much you think you're prepared and have all the bases covered, when someone is obsessed with you, deranged and obsessed with you, you're all they think about. And they always manage to stay a step ahead and get too close."

"That happened to you?" I try to keep my voice even.

He brushes hair behind my ear and searches my face for a moment before going on.

"One of them was so obsessed, she was delusional. Thought we were destined to be together." He shakes his head and blows out a heavy breath. "It was sad, but got pretty out of control. She would pop up at the studio. She'd wait at the community gate. Wherever I was she somehow managed to be there too. That's actually when I started with the disguises. We got a restraining order, and the police were involved every step of the way. She even went into counseling, and for a while, everything was fine. Then one day I came downstairs and she was just standing there in my kitchen holding one of the knives."

"Oh, God, Rhys." Even though I know he's safe, fear chills my skin and staccatos my breath. "What happened?"

"I just tried to keep her talking." He shakes his head. "It was only a few minutes. She didn't realize she had tripped the alarm. It sent a silent signal to the cops before it kicked in. When the alarm started blaring, she put the knife to her wrist, but I knocked it out of her hands. We struggled a little, but I was much bigger and stronger than she was."

His eyes go unfocused for a second like he's standing back in that kitchen still struggling with her.

"The cops showed up really quickly," he says, "And they took her away. I never heard anything more except that she was getting the help she needed."

The thought of this crazy woman getting that close, finding a way inside a home I've always believed impenetrable, makes me feel sick.

"Could it be her?" I ask. "I mean, could she be the one who left the shirt and the message?"

"No, Gep already checked. She's still in the facility she went to after that last incident." He narrows his eyes. "No, this is someone else. But I can't let my guard down like I did before. Especially not now that I have you."

He dots kisses along my hairline and kisses my ring finger, bright with the symbol of the life we've chosen together.

"If anything ever happened to you because of me, Kai . . ." His convulsive gulp swallows the rest of that thought. "I couldn't live with that. I wouldn't . . . to even think about it—"

"Nothing's gonna happen to me." I lay my palm against the strong angle of his jaw. "Or to you."

"Don't worry about me." He turns his lips into my palm. "I can take care of myself."

"And I can't take care of myself?" I rear back to chastise his double standard.

"I'm sure you could." He smiles and lifts my left hand, caressing the band of my engagement ring. "But this says I get to take care of you now. This says you're mine."

"Oh, and what says you're mine?" Some of the tension eases from my shoulders the longer we smile and whisper to each other, walling out the world.

His smile fades a little and his eyes grow more serious. He takes my hand and presses it against his chest until his heartbeat thuds into my palm like a fervent bass drum.

"This does." He marries our fingers over his chest. "My heart and every other part of me says I'm yours. I love you, Pep, more than anything in this world."

Perfect love casts out fear.

I don't know why that simple phrase, like a relic from my past, gives me any confidence, but it does. We won't run and hide from a threat we know so little about. Maybe it's true that love and fear can't occupy the same space. Maybe my father was right. It wouldn't be the first time. Despite my resentment and lingering bitterness over his abandonment, I have the feeling it won't be the last.

"Let's go to Vegas." I inject the fledgling confidence into my voice, into my eyes. I want him to see that I'm fearless. That I want to be with him, and no one, especially not some deranged twat with the twisted idea that he belongs to her, will keep me from being where I belong. Not just on stage, but by his side.

He searches my face, brushes a thumb over my cheekbone and sighs, resignation stealing over his face inch by inch. He sighs deeply before leaving a kiss to my forehead and pressing me to his chest.

"Okay, babe. We'll go."

11

ai

IT'S NOT MORNING SICKNESS SWIRLING NAUSEA in my stomach. The eggs and cheese and vegetables of my omelet may as well be tar in my mouth. Every time I try to swallow, I see that shirt again, slashed and covered in pig's blood. I feel that blood soaking through my tank top and sticking to my skin. See it washing crimson down the drain of our shower from my body and from my hands. I've been reciting my little verse, leaning on it for strength, but ever since we arrived in Vegas, the comfort I drew from the words seems dimmer. I keep trying to recapture that confidence, but for whatever reason, being here in Vegas has made it harder.

So here we sit at The Park, the high-end hotel where the showcase will be held tomorrow night. It's one of the newest and most extravagant hotels on the Strip. The Parker Group owns hotels all over the world, but they've just added Vegas. Hosting our showcase here is a real coup. We arrived at different times last night, so Bristol's using this breakfast to brief everyone about the agenda, which is full. I know I need to eat, but I can't seem to manage more than a few bites before I'm assaulted by the smell of that blood and the stickiness on my palms.

"Pep, you okay?" Rhyson leans close to ask. "You're not eating. Is it morning sickness?"

I glance around the table to make sure no one heard him. Rhyson and I agreed to keep the pregnancy to ourselves until we're closer to the second trimester.

"I'm fine." I hope my smile looks genuine, but I can tell by the concern on his face he knows something is off. "Guess I'm not hungry."

"If it's morning sickness, then—"

"Shhh." I make sure everyone else is paying attention to Bristol and not to us. "What happened to keeping it quiet?"

"You're right." Rhyson nods and continues with a slightly softer tone. "I have some meds, though, in case you need something."

I turn surprised eyes his way.

"What?" He shrugs like it's normal for him to carry nausea pills for pregnant women. "I asked Dr. Allister for recommendations, just in case."

"How-what-why?" I shake my head, confused. "When did you ask Dr. Allister?"

"We chatted after the appointment while you were getting dressed. She gave me her cell number." He tosses a blueberry into his mouth. "She told me to call her anytime, night or day."

"I just bet she did," I grumble. "I guess the whole rock star thing comes in handy sometimes."

He offers me a pitying glance over his orange juice like I couldn't be more wrong.

"Pep, come on. She's a professional, not a fan, and just doing her job."

"Somehow I don't think she's giving most patients her personal cell number. I—"

"So sorry to interrupt," Bristol sprinkles sarcasm like the powdered sugar on her French toast, "But do you two have something you'd like to share with the rest of the class?"

Rhys and I exchange a chagrined look before giving Bristol our undivided attention.

"Thank you." She looks pointedly from her iPad to Kai. "What I was trying to say is that Ella arrived and is already in your suite setting up. She'll get you ready for the meet and greet."

"Oh, good." There's so much testosterone since I'm the only girl, it'll be nice to have another chick around.

"For the meet and greet at noon, you'll each have your own table." Bristol gives her brother a wary glance. "Rhyson, you might not like this, but hear me out."

"Listening." He folds his arms across his chest and waits.

"I've separated everyone into their own quadrant so there's plenty of space to accommodate your lines." Her shoulders are already squared and braced for his response.

"I'm at Kai's table." Rhyson returns to his meal like a debate isn't about to ensue.

"That doesn't make sense, Rhys." Bristol slumps back in her seat and leans her forehead into her hand. "Your lines will be longer than everyone's. You need the most space, and I've already arranged a separate quadrant for you."

"Then unarrange it." Rhyson fixes his sister with a stony stare. "You're lucky we're even here. Whoever left that shirt on my car is still out there, and we're no closer to finding them than we were last week when it happened. I'm not leaving Kai that vulnerable with so many people unless I'm right there."

"Don't overreact. We've dealt with stalkers before," Bristol reasons. "You know how this works."

"I've had stalkers before, yes," Rhyson says. "But I didn't have Kai before."

My cheeks burn under everyone's sudden attention. I try to smile, fail, and settle for spearing a mushroom with my fork.

"Gep, please talk some sense into him." Bristol rolls her eyes and takes a bite of her eggs.

"We'll have someone from the team at Kai's table, Rhys," Gep's gruff voice tries to soothe.

"I don't give a damn what you'll have," Rhyson explodes, his fork clanking loudly on the plate when he tosses it down.

The table, everyone seated around it—Grip, the guys from Kilimanjaro, Luke—all go silent, dropping their eyes to the remains of their breakfast. A cautious glance around the room confirms that other people are staring. They know who he is, who I am, who we all are.

"Guys, if you're done, Tammi, our new assistant, is upstairs in my suite waiting for us." Bristol's smile is a fraud betrayed by the anger in her eyes. "I'll meet you upstairs in a little bit."

The guys from the band stand and make their way to the elevators. Luke and Grip linger a few moments longer. They're not just Prodigy artists. They're Rhyson's friends, and their concern is evident in the careful way they watch him.

"You sure you okay, man?" Grip's serious demeanor is at odds with his typical good humor.

"Yeah. I'm cool." Rhys nods jerkily and splits a look between Grip and Luke. "I'm not trying to be an asshole, I just . . .

His words fade and his eyes shift to me. I don't know if they detect the helplessness, the fear hiding under Rhyson's frustration, but I do. It took a lot to get him here, and now that we are here, the same second thoughts seem to be assailing him that plague me. I reach for his hand under the table and give what I hope is a reassuring squeeze.

"Hey, we're used to it." Luke laughs and chips away at some of the tension encircling the table. "If you weren't being an asshole, we'd be worried."

Rhyson surrenders to a natural smile and fist pounds them both.

"We'll see you upstairs." Grip nods toward the elevators.

Luke bends to drop a kiss on my hair and whispers in my ear, "Hang in there, kiddo."

I smile up into his blue eyes before returning my attention to the combatants seated at the table. Gep and I are simply innocent bystanders and possible referees at this point.

"If you could refrain from making fools of us all," Bristol says, irritation creasing her pretty face, "I'd really appreciate that. The last thing we need is bad publicity right before tomorrow's showcase."

"I don't give a damn about publicity, Bris." Annoyance tautens the skin over Rhyson's high cheekbones.

"What a shame since that is the absolute point of this trip." Bristol leans forward, lowers her voice, and levels her eyes on her twin brother. "We've worked hard, Kai included, to get ready for this showcase. I understand you don't have anything left to prove or to lose, but these guys do. Each of them signed with Prodigy trusting you to make decisions in their best interests. Don't abuse that."

"I would never." Rhyson scowls down at his plate. "I'm not."

"You have a responsibility to all the people who are working hard to get Prodigy off the ground," Bristol continues, undaunted, "Who put their futures in your hands."

"When have I ever neglected that responsibility?" Rhyson's eyes clash with Bristol's across the table. "But I also have a responsibility to protect Kai."

"Rhyson, I'll be fine." I say it to reassure him, but there is a part of me that is not fine. The part that can't take a bite of my omelet without smelling blood and tasting fear.

"I know you will because I'll be right there with you." Nothing about Rhyson's face yields. "Bris, it's not a big deal. There's too much left out of my . . . out of our control. Maybe it won't make a difference, but it will make me feel better."

She should just give him what he wants. I honestly don't care if he's at the table with me or not. Rhyson's female fans probably won't be thrilled to see his fiancée there as part of the package, but they'll get over it.

"Compromise. Separate tables in the same quadrant." Bristol raises her brows into a perfectly arched question. "Deal?"

Rhyson nods reluctantly, wordlessly.

"Now that wasn't so hard, was it?" Bristol sips her mimosa, humor suddenly lighting up her eyes. "My life would be so boringly perfect if we didn't have these occasional battles."

"Well, I don't need the drama." His face relaxes and he forks a square of French toast to his lips. "So just give me what I want without a fight every once in a while."

Gep and I surreptitiously exchange the look we've shared on more than one occasion when the siblings fight. The storms blow through so hard and fast with these two. They'd do anything for each other, but sometimes it seems they fight just so they don't get out of practice.

"Eat just a little more, Pep." Rhyson aims his fork at my still-full plate.

"I'm not that hungry."

Rhyson stops mid-chew, assessing my face.

"You sure you feel up to all this today?" Concern narrows and darkens his eyes. "It's going to be really hot."

"We'll be inside."

"There'll be lots of people."

"Won't be the first time."

He dips his head until his mouth caresses my ear and his words are only mine.

"If we skip, we could make love on the balcony, fifty stories up," he rasps against my neck, stirring urges we don't have time to indulge. "Someone might see."

I turn my head until our noses touch. Ignoring Gep, Bristol and anyone in the dining room who might give a damn, I touch my lips to his. It's just a brush of lips, so tender and hot and sweet that a lump fills my throat. I have no idea where this feeling comes from except this connection always simmers between us, waiting for the slightest touch to flare to life. It affects him too. He makes a hungry sound in the back of his throat, following me with his lips when I pull back. He cups my neck, his fingers wandering into my hair. His mouth settles over mine, chaste to any observer, but rich with our private passion.

"I've always felt this way about you," he whispers, his eyes so warm my skin heats. "It started the moment I saw you. It was smaller then, but there has never been a time when you didn't affect me more deeply than anyone else ever has."

"Why do you think that is?" I whisper back, glancing across the table to find Bristol and Gep reviewing the security team's plans for the meet and greet.

"I've never quite understood it myself." His eyes are alive with laughter and bottomless affection. "Lucky for us we've got the rest of our lives to figure it out."

12

ai

"I LIKE YOUR HAIR LIKE THIS."

I turn my head toward Rhyson's softly spoken compliment. He's leaning into the corner of the elevator, Gep a few feet to his left. His full lips tip up at one corner as he eyes the hair falling from a deep side part, bone straight and past my shoulders.

"Thank you." I nod to Ella, who styled me and is riding down with us to the meet and greet. "He likes your handiwork, lady."

Rhyson's lazy grin creases his lean cheeks and warms his eyes.

"You did her hair for the birthday party too, right?" he asks. "I liked it like that, too."

"How do you like Kai's hair best?" Ella winks at me.

Rhyson lifts and drops a few strands of the hair clinging to my bare arm, his eyes darkening to slate.

"On my pillow." He laughs and shrugs when I cover my reddening face with both hands. "What? She asked!"

I widen my eyes at him and avoid amused looks from Ella and Gep. Around floor thirty-eight, a gentle hand tugs me back to stand against Rhyson's chest. My breath stutters at the heat of our proximity. He pushes my hair aside, his breath fluttering over the sensitive skin of my neck. The anticipation of his touch layers tension across my body.

Limb by limb, my shoulders, arms, butt, and legs melt into him. A sharply drawn breath at my ear confirms I'm not alone in this sweet torture. I may be softer in all the places he's firm, but he's as much putty in my hands as I am in his. The clean, masculine scent, so uniquely his, wraps around me. A shiver skitters down my spine when his fingers brush against my skin ostensibly to close the button of the dress Ella brought to the suite earlier, a sleeveless linen shift that skims my curves and flares around my thighs. Colored polka dots create cheery pops of color against the white palette.

"Your button came loose." Rhyson's words are innocent enough, but I hear the throb embedded in the huskiness of his voice.

"Thank you." I angle my head to catch his eyes over my shoulder. Will it ever get old, this bolt of sensation transmitted between us when our eyes meet? I force myself to look away before the connection deepens beyond what I can handle in the bounds of decency and the confines of an elevator.

Ella attempts small talk with Gep, and they're so close I'm surprised they don't smell passion thickening the air. Rhyson and I remain silent during the descent, relishing the secret brewing between our bodies. The ding of the elevator finally landing at the lobby snaps into the taut air around us. Even the few steps I take forward to exit the elevator don't erase the shape of him imprinted into my back.

"Damn." Rhyson pats the pockets of his dark jeans. "I left my phone upstairs. Gep, go with Kai, and I'll meet you guys there."

Gep doesn't look too pleased about abandoning his post. Considering all of Rhyson's fans sure to be milling around in the lobby, neither am I.

"It's like what, a hundred feet from here to the table?" I turn Gep back toward the elevator by his shoulder. "Gep can stay with you. I'll be fine."

"That's not an option, Pep." If Rhyson's words didn't just tell me I'm not taking even those hundred feet alone, the deep scowl on his face does.

"I'll just text one of the guys to meet you at the penthouse." Gep is already typing on his phone.

Before I can protest any further, the elevator doors are closing on Rhyson's smug smile, and he's gone. Gep, Ella, and I head toward the area Bristol designated for Rhyson and me to meet and greet.

"On my pillow." Ella's whisper hides the words from Gep's alert ears. "Gah, how do you not just melt all over that man? The way he looks at you and the things he says. I'd be a puddle, and he'd basically have to carry me around in a glass all day."

Laugher sputters over my lips at the image of Rhyson transporting a liquid Ella in a tumbler.

"He is pretty dreamy." The trusty lovesick smile takes over my face. "Sometimes I—"

"Kai!" someone calls from a few feet away.

I turn toward my name, and surprise glues my feet to the lobby's expensive carpet.

"Dub." I shake my head, forcing myself to orient and recover. "Hey. What are you doing here?"

"I was hoping we'd run into each other." That's not exactly an answer to my question, and we both know it. A silence falls between us, and I'm not sure what to fill it with.

"I'm gonna go check on the guys and make sure they're all presentable." Ella's smile doesn't hide her curiosity. "Later, Dub. Good seeing you again."

As soon as she's out of earshot, the words rush out of me.

"Dub, why are you here?"

Dub's eyes flick to Gep standing like a stone sentry at my side. I've gotten so used to having security around us all the time, especially Gep, I forget he's even there sometimes. They become like the wallpaper. If wallpaper knows a dozen ways to kill you and efficiently dispose of the body.

"Gep, could you give us a second?" Impatience compresses my mouth when he doesn't move. "It's okay. You know we're friends."

Gep's eyes remind me that he knows more than just about anyone else, including how displeased the man who signs his paycheck would be. With a look that asks if I'm sure about this, he takes a measly two steps away.

"I know it sounds conceited but I have to ask." An anxious breath slips out. "You're not here for me, are you? This is just a coincidence?"

"I knew the showcase was this weekend." Dub shrugs, his muscular shoulders straining against his t-shirt. "Your cell wasn't working, so I was hoping to catch you without Gray's goons, but I see he keeps you as locked down here as he does in LA."

"I'm not locked down." I press fingers to my temple, already anticipating a headache. "Rhyson's on his way down. You should go."

"Why? It's a free country."

"But I'm not free, Dub." My voice softens for the man who was such a good friend to me on tour until he started asking for more. "I'm engaged. You know that, right?"

"Oh, he made sure I'd know." Bitterness deepens his Irish lilt and distorts his chuckle into a bark. "He was sending me a message. A man as private as Gray wouldn't make such a show of something that personal without a good reason."

I won't tell Dub that he's flattering himself if he thinks Rhyson's public proposal had anything to do with him.

"Please go before he sees you."

"Are you afraid of him, Kai?" One large hand wraps around my elbow, and the other presses into my hip, drawing me a few inches closer. "Is that it?"

"Afraid of Rhys?" I scoff and tug unsuccessfully to loosen my elbow. "Of course not. Please let me go before he comes. I don't want a scene. I have this meet and greet today and the showcase tomorrow. I need to focus, and I don't know what else to do to make it clear this can't happen."

"I miss you, Kai." He dips to hold my eyes, the massive shoulders blocking everything behind him. "I miss working with you. I know the choreographer you used for Grip's video. You can't tell me you have the same chemistry with her that you have with me."

"It's not about that, Dub." I sigh and glance at Gep, who is eyeing Dub's hand on my arm. "You're right. We have great artistic chemistry, but your . . . feelings make things complicated."

"You care about me." He grips my chin, leaning so close his breath whispers across my lips. "You miss me. I know you do."

I shake my head, as much to free my chin from his fingers as to deny his mistaken assumption. Did I miss working with him on Grip's shoot? Miss feeling like another dancer could read my mind with his choreography? Miss the moves that felt tailor-made for my body? Yes, of course. But that pales in comparison to what I gain letting go of Dub. Rhyson's trust. His appreciation that I put us first.

"Dub, we're friends. I do care about you. Of course, I do, but . . ."

The half-formed sentence trails off as I search for the right words. It's because I care that I need to get him out of here before Rhyson comes. In the pause I use to make sure I can be firm and tactful without being cruel, a familiar weight settles at the small of my back. A large hand, tipped with calluses from making beautiful music, pulls me away from Dub.

Daggumit.

"Dub." Rhyson's voice is a dirty cocktail of tolerance and disdain. "I had no idea this town was so small. Imagine running into you like this. You here for a shoot?"

"Nope." Defiance glints in Dub's eyes.

"Oh." Rhyson draws me deeper into the cove of his body. "Party? Meeting? Vacation?"

"Nope." Dub glances from Rhyson's possessive hold on me and back to his face. "None of the above."

The corners of Rhyson's mouth turn down, appropriate since I know that's the direction this conversation is headed.

"Kai, I think Bristol's looking for you. We'll be getting started soon." He drops a kiss into my hair and turns to Gep. "Could you take her to our table, Gep? I think it's just around the corner."

"Rhys, come with me." I wrap my hand around his strong wrist. "Most of the people will be your fans. You don't want to keep them waiting."

"The first in line will have been waiting for a long time. A few more minutes won't make much difference." He slides hard eyes in Dub's direction. "Besides this won't take long."

"Rhyson, don't—"

He doesn't offer words to stop my protest. He silences me with a glance. A blizzard of fury, cold and unrelenting, falls in his eyes when he turns to stare at me. I wanted to spare Dub this, but he's brought it on himself really. And if it comes down to creating tension with the man I love or leaving Dub to his own dumb devices, I'll choose the man I love every time. I can only hope that Rhyson will show some mercy.

"Gep, let's go." I turn and leave Dub with the tiger he just poked.

13

Rhsyon

THIS BREAKDANCING MOTHERFUCKER NEVER LEARNS.

He has no idea how high I am on the bat shit meter right now. I saw him as soon as I stepped off the elevator. Saw him pawing my girl's arm. Saw her try to pull away. Saw him holding on. He's going to lose that hand if he's not careful. But when I look back at Dub, I don't see a careful man. I see a desperate one. His feelings for Kai must go even deeper than I thought for him to come here like this. It makes me want to crush him into a paste of unfulfilled ambition and broken dreams. It makes me want to take everything from him for his audacity thinking he could ever take her away from me.

"Did you come here to see Kai?" My calm voice belies the anger bubbling under my skin.

"I needed to talk to her."

"Well, you have, and now you won't again. If you keep popping up in places you don't belong and touching things that aren't yours, there might be consequences."

"Like what?" He folds tree stump arms over his wide chest. "What kinds of things could happen, Gray? Tell me."

"Well, seems to me it takes more than talent to make it in this industry. It's also who you know."

"Your point?"

"Well, Jimi was your inroad to all of this. Based on what I can see, nearly every client you've worked with was directly or indirectly connected to her."

"Again, your point?"

"What if Jimi all of a sudden wasn't satisfied with your work? Couldn't vouch for you? Maybe Luke expresses some dissatisfaction with what you did for his tour. Maybe you're hard to work with. Unreliable. You never know. We artists are so fickle."

"Are you threatening me?" He steamrolls past his own question before I can respond. "You arrogant son of a bitch."

"Ding, ding, ding!" I tap my nose. "Ladies and gentlemen, I think he finally gets it. Yes, I'm an arrogant son of a bitch who usually gets what I want. And what I want is for you to stay the hell away from my fiancée. If you don't, you'll be blackballed and dancing at theme parks before the year is out. And we're not talking Disney."

"What would Kai say if she knew you were threatening me like this?"

"You think she doesn't?" My laugh is genuine because he really has no clue. "You think I hide myself from her? I don't. She knows exactly who I am. That I am, as you said, an arrogant son of a bitch, and she loves me anyway. Why do you think she was trying to get you out of here, dumbass? She's your friend, and though you don't seem to understand the boundaries of friendship, she does. And as your friend, she didn't want it to come to this."

"Are you sure you want to hold Jimi over my head?" A calculating gleam enters his eyes. "I mean, she and I may want the same things."

"Not sure what you mean." I know exactly where this prick is headed.

"Let's just say Jimi's a very forthcoming drunk." He cackles. "But you'd know more about her 'coming' than I would."

"Kai knows I fucked Jimi. That happened before she and I even met." I tilt my head to consider him. "If this is your version of a threat, I'm just gonna tell you it leaves a lot to be desired."

I watch realization morph into disappointment. That's all he's got? Damn. Amateur hour.

"This is your last warning." I step closer so my words have less distance to travel before they land on him. He's bulkier and I'm taller, but it's not height or muscle that determines the balance of power between us. "Here's what I can promise you. The next time you pull some stupid shit like this, you'll regret it."

"I care about her, Gray." His teeth cage the words. His jaw clenches. "I don't want to see her hurt."

"And you think I would hurt her?"

"You have before," he says. "You want to control her. I heard enough from that video of your fight to know it's all about control with you. I know you boxed me out of her career to control her. You don't deserve her."

"You think I don't know that?" I grind out.

"Guys like you—"

"I'm completely in love with her. No matter what you've heard about me and my past, that's all you need to know." His startled eyes find mine. "You think I'd ask her to marry me in front of the whole world if I wasn't crazy about her?"

"She and I make a great team. You shouldn't stand in the way of that."

"Look me in the eye and tell me you don't want to fuck my girl." Even just saying the words spikes my pulse and pummels my reason to powder.

He looks me in the eye, but doesn't say a word. His silent admission curls my hands into fists at my side.

"It'll never happen." Each word is sharp and cold like a chip of ice. "I would destroy you before that would ever happen."

"Idle threats don't scare me, Gray."

"What about real ones? Because I mean every fucking word."

"Kai and I have a connection." His eyes don't leave my face. "You've seen it. That's why you keep us apart."

"I didn't sabotage your working relationship with Kai. You did that by getting your dick involved. She'll choose me every time, Dub. And I'll choose her over every other thing that means anything to me because nothing will ever mean more to me than she does."

He goes silent, looking down at the floor and then around the lobby. I glance at my watch, realizing this is taking more time than I have. If I listen hard enough I'm sure I'll hear Bristol screaming bloody murder.

"Look, Dub, I'm not gonna waste any more time defending my relationship with Kai or trying to prove my feelings to you. You don't matter enough for that. Whatever you imagine being with Kai is like, I guarantee you it's a million times better. And if you think I'm giving that up, you're dumber than I thought."

Our eyes connect, and I don't know if it's pain or anger in his gaze, but it's a strong emotion. It's real. He really does care for her, which only escalates my irritation.

"Go home," I snap. "Or wherever. I don't care, but you will stay away from my girl."

I don't wait to see if my words get through to him or not, but turn and walk in the direction Gep and Kai took a few minutes ago. She's standing there as soon as I round the corner, biting her thumbnail. Anxiety tightens like a mask on her face. My hand strokes at the tension knotting her delicate jawline. Her eyes move like a searchlight across my face.

"What did you say to him?" She lays her hand over mine where it cradles her face. "Please don't hurt him."

Her words clamp my teeth together. Between the desire I saw in his eyes for her and the plea I read in her eyes for him, the thin thread my civility was hanging by snaps. I glance around until I spot a nook just beyond the pre-conference area. I grab her arm, keeping my grip firm, but gentle, and start toward the nook and a measure of privacy. I can see the line of fans already formed just beyond the glass door Bristol hasn't opened yet.

"Gep, don't let Bristol open that door until I say so." I glance at him and urge her ahead of me. "Don't let anyone back here."

"You got it, boss." His face gives away nothing.

As soon as we make it into the darkened space, I press her into the wall beside a stack of chairs.

"Rhyson, we need to get back out there." She swallows, her dark eyes climbing over my chest and shoulders, skimming the straight line of my mouth before finally reaching my eyes. I don't speak, but lean my hips into her, letting her feel how hard I am.

"He came here for you, Kai," I growl, a breath shy of her lips. "He wants to convince you that you shouldn't be with me."

"Dub—"

"Don't say his fucking name." Fury tremors through me. Without thought for the fans just beyond the door, or for Gep a few feet past the wall, I slip my fingers under her dress and into her panties. My thumb circles her clit, and I'm rewarded by her gasp. Unceremoniously, I insinuate my middle finger inside her.

"Rhyson." My name breaks on a ragged breath even as her hips rotate into my hand and her eyelids drop.

"Is it mine?" My thumb is merciless, pressing and rubbing the little knot of flesh-covered nerves between her legs.

"God, yes." Her head thumps against the wall, her lashes at half-mast over the want in her eyes. "But we have to stop. Bristol will be furious."

"I'm furious." My voice gravels with lust and frustration. "He thinks he can take this from me."

"You know he can't," she pants. "You know I'm yours. We don't have time for this, baby."

Her words say that, but her body begs to differ. Her nipples pebble beneath the dress. Her mouth goes slack with the pleasure I'm stroking to life. Her legs spread just the tiniest bit when I add another finger, steadily penetrating, my mouth hovering over hers and eating her desperate cries.

"Let me hear you," I rub my nose into her neck. Her skin is satin and her scent confiscates my breath.

"Gep's too close."

"I don't care if he hears." In that moment, it's true. I need to hear her surrender. I need the affirmation that she's mine pouring hot and wet on my fingers. I need to see her fall apart for me. For me. Dub's right. I don't deserve her, but I'll be damned if he'll have her. I don't know what I'd do to anyone who tried to take her from me.

"Oh, my God." She clenches around my fingers like a silk knot and slumps against the wall, her hips still jerking over my hand. Her cries wash over me, and I drop my forehead to hers. Our lips mesh, my hand still under her dress. I lick deeply into her mouth, and she parries, her sweet little tongue answering me. She grips me through my jeans, squeezing my stiffened length. We're lost in this storm, and I can't find my way back out. The waiting fans, the pressures, none of it reaches me. Only her. Only Kai. My emotions have swung on a pendulum the last hour, veering wildly from jealousy and anger to this love that's wide enough to lose myself in and narrowed down to just one girl. Forever.

Marry me.

The words spontaneously combust in my mind and simmer on the tip of my tongue, bolstered by the emotions stewing inside me. It's a fully-formed, perfect thought. The idea of us getting married right away. Of her being Mrs. Rhyson Gray when she has our baby and before the sun goes down. I know she'll think it's connected to the drama with Dub, but it's not. I'll get her to understand.

"Pep, let's—"

"Rhyson, what the hell." Bristol's angry voice reaches around the corner like a rubber arm. "Gep, you better let me by."

Shit.

"Fuck Vegas," I mutter with my temple pressed into the wall beside Kai's.

Tiny vibrations echo from her body to mine. When I glance down, her full lips press tight against the laughter brimming from her eyes. I give her a slow grin, relishing our last moments alone before the circus comes to town.

"Rhyson, I will junk punch Gep to get to you." Bristol sounds completely serious, and I wouldn't put it past her. Gep and his junk would never forgive me.

"Bris, don't come back here." I turn my head in the direction of her threat. "We're coming."

"I need both of you like five minutes ago. Another group has our space later, and the staff will need time to turn it around before the next event starts. There's a ton of crap going on today. It's gonna be a madhouse."

"We're coming."

I realize my fingers are still buried inside Kai. Now that we're out of the moment, self-consciousness stains her cheeks pink, and she bites her lip. I take my time pulling my fingers out, caressing her from the inside as I go.

"We'll finish this later." I roll the wet fingers in my mouth, savoring her like an appetizer.

She shudders, her eyes flitting closed for a second before she pulls a shaking hand through her hair.

"What happened with Dub?" she asks softly.

"We talked." I braid our fingers together and pull her into my chest.

"Don't hurt him, Rhys." She lifts her lashes and watches me steadily.

"I won't." I brush my knuckle over her cheekbone. "As long as he stays away. If he pulls this shit again, I'll do whatever it takes to make him understand. Don't ask me not to protect this. Not to protect us."

She glances at our fingers twined against my chest and nods. After a few seconds she walks away to face Bristol and the waiting crowd. Once I round the corner, there's a line of people with t-shirts, CDs, magazines, and other items to be signed. I don't do this often, give this level of access to fans. So when I do, it's three-ring madness. At least this time I have Kai by my side. Technically, at the table nearby. Sitting across from her for the next few hours, but unable to really connect will be torture, but at least I'll be right there to make sure she's safe. At least we'll be in it together.

14

ai

I'LL HAVE TO SCRAPE THIS SMILE off my face when this is over. And if I have to sign one more autograph, my hand may just detach and walk off in protest. Sharing a space with Rhyson is unlike any other experience I've had. We had meet and greets after shows on Luke's tour. We did mall appearances. Malcolm even arranged a showcase once for all of his artists, very similar to this one. Except this one features Rhyson Gray. And I'm witnessing the fervor of his fans up close.

So many celebrities pretend they don't want the attention and just love the music. Rhyson actually lives that way with his disguises and practically hibernating in the studio. He wants to walk outside, to live his life and not be recognized, not be bothered. But this is the trade-off for his passion to perform and create, so he lives with it. As I watch the line of people waiting for hours just to get a moment with him, I know Rhyson would never choose this. Never seek this. Too much of it would be soul-eating for him.

I still don't know what happened with him and Dub, but it couldn't have been great for Rhyson to respond the way he did. Every once in a while, our eyes catch and hold. The tumultuous memories of the heated moments in that corridor spark between us before we each return to autographs and fans. A shiver writhes up my spine and I cross my legs to contain the fire he started in my panties. My imagination is inescapable, though. My memory of his fingers working inside me, of his eyes watching my body intently for signs of surrender—faultless.

"Everything okay over here?" Bristol comes to stand beside me, inspecting the mass of people still waiting to see Rhyson. "Looks like you're done. So's everyone else."

"As you can see," I say, tipping my head in the direction of his seemingly never-ending line. "He's not."

Rhyson stands to take a few pictures. A clump of people rush forward at once, disturbing the orderly flow of things. My heart cramps in my chest for the few moments I can't see more of him than the top of his dark head.

"I think we need to shut this down, Bristol." My words come out strained. Ever since Rhyson told me the story about the stalker standing in his kitchen with a knife, I've felt as fiercely protective of him as he must feel of me. Maybe we shouldn't have come. I want to lock him away in our bedroom and not share any part of him with these people.

"I think you're right." Bristol walks over and whispers to Gep, who nods and signals one of his team members to move closer to Rhyson. I move too. The longer he's standing in that crowd unprotected and vulnerable, the sweatier my palms become. I press my way through the knot of fans until I'm at his side. I casually hook my elbow through his. He looks down at me, smiles, and gives me a quick kiss.

When I look up, I encounter a set of blue eyes boiling with

suppressed emotion. It's directed at me. I know it. A frisson, some ancient sense, warns me about the girl standing a few feet away. It's just an exchange we make with our eyes, but I've never felt more certain of danger. All the other faces are eager, starstruck. Hers is resentful, like I took something from her. She's a few inches away when I see something shiny glint in her hand. I don't think. I don't rationalize. Fear and the need to protect Rhyson set me in motion before I can work out a plan or strategize. I press my back to his chest, inserting myself between him and that resentment, between him and the girl, and I shove my hand as hard as I can into her chest. She stumbles back and falls. All around I hear gasps, startled sounds at what I've done.

"Kai, what the hell?" Rhyson looks at me, confusion sparking in his grey eyes.

He reaches down to help the young woman to her feet. Even with all eyes on me, wondering what happened, I want to rip her hand from his. I want to urge him not to get too close. I look for the shiny item I saw her gripping. It's a pen. A silver pen probably for an autograph. God, I'm being paranoid and feel like an idiot.

"So sorry about that." Bristol rushes in for damage control. "Just an accident."

"She pushed me." The girl's eyes run hot with anger in the pale, narrow face. It mottles her skin.

"She didn't mean to." Bristol aims a meaningful glance my way, silently compelling me to agree. "Right, Kai?"

"Um, yes. I'm so sorry," I mumble. "It was an accident. I hope you're okay. I apologize."

"No, you pushed me." The girl's eyes never leave my face, and her voice doesn't yield. She won't be soothed. She and I both know it was no accident.

"No, I'm sure it was an accident." Rhyson pats her shoulder and bends to her height so he can look right in her eyes, his effortless charm finally breaking through that resentment. Her expression softens until she's smiling at him.

"Tell you what," Rhyson says. "Do you have tickets for the showcase tomorrow?"

The girl shakes her head, eagerness replacing the resentment and anger.

"Bristol, let's get her two tickets." Rhyson widens his smile for her. "Just to show how sorry we are."

He subtly elbows me in the ribs.

"Uh, yes," I manage to say. "So sorry. My mistake for, um . . . stumbling into you."

Her smile calcifies a little when our eyes meet.

"No problem," she says. "I understand."

"Everyone, thank you for being so patient." Bristol raises her voice so as many people in the line as possible can hear. "But Rhyson has to rehearse. He'll be available for a few minutes after tomorrow night's showcase. Hope to see you then."

Rhyson grasps my elbow firmly, catches Gep's eyes, and jerks his head toward the penthouse elevator. We're practically marching, and I'm tripping over my dignity trying to keep up with him.

"Slow down, Rhys," I say weakly. I figure he's thrown by the incident, but I'll fall if he doesn't let up.

As soon as the elevator doors close, I expect him to let loose whatever pulls his lips into a thin line and bunches his hands into fists by his side, but he's silent, eyes trained on the ascending illuminated numbers. Impatience rolls off him, like he'd climb the elevator shaft himself if that would get us there faster. Once we reach the penthouse level, he recaptures my arm and drags me to our suite.

"Gep, we're fine," he flings over his shoulder. "You can go."

"I'll stay out here, if that's okay." Gep glances up and down the corridor.

"It's not okay." Rhyson breaks stride to face his security team lead, matching him frown for frown. "No one can even access this floor without a key. Go. I'll call you if we decide to leave."

Gep hesitates before turning to press the elevator button.

On the other side of our door, the opulence of the suite fades into oblivion. Diffusing this tension absorbs all my focus and energy.

"Rhys, I can explain."

"You don't have to explain." His eyes slice into me. "You pushed her."

"Yes." I nod, unable and unwilling to lie to him. "But I thought—"

"That she was going to hurt me. I know. I could tell by how you shoved me aside like some bodyguard before you pushed the poor girl to the floor."

My mouth slams closed over the defenses and excuses queued up in my throat.

"Well, yes, but I—"

"And you thought the thing to do if someone was threatening me was to put yourself in danger. To put our child in danger." His false calm barely veneers the emotion fuming underneath. "That made sense to you, right?"

"I didn't think," I admit softly. I hadn't. The baby didn't even occur to me. My own life didn't occur to me. Only protecting him.

"You're damn right, you didn't think." His voice erupts into the empty room. "Fuck, Kai! Don't ever do that again."

Anxiety has left a film of perspiration over my skin. I'm stuck in a pot boiling over with his anger and frustration. I stride toward the kitchen to find escape and a bottle of water.

"Do not walk away from me." His voice gains ground on me until he's standing in the kitchen like a shadow. "This conversation isn't over."

"It is if you're gonna ask me to do anything differently next time." I address my words to the suite refrigerator. Residual panic still heats my face and shoulders. I stand in the open door and revel in the artificially cool air.

I turn, bottle of water in hand, to find him right there, blocking my path. His arms rise on either side of my head, trapping me against the stainless steel door.

"Rhys."

His name leaves me on a breath. He's so much bigger than I am. So close. An aura of desperation vibrates around him. I'm caught in it like a web, a silken trap I want to twist myself deeper into. I'm inappropriately turned on by the force of it. Any sane woman would be frightened by the intensity of the silvered eyes blaring his frustration. Of the corded forearms like bars imprisoning me against a major appliance. But I know he would never hurt me, and all I can think about is how all that raw emotion would feel exploding inside me. Unleashed on me. How he would ruin me from the inside out. How I would love every second of it.

"Did it ever occur to you that I thought she was a threat too?" The hot breath fueling his words singes my lips. Makes me burn brighter. "That in those few seconds where you were scared for me, I was scared out of my mind for you?"

I lift my eyes to his, stripping away the outer skin of his frustration, biting through the flesh of his anger, until there at the core, I see it. Fear. It's a dark note we both hear, a dissonant chord connecting us.

"How would I live with myself if a knife, a bullet, any threat meant for me, hurt you?" His voice cracks, and he closes his eyes, shuttering that fear, but I still feel it. With his forehead dropped to mine, it seeps through my skin. Sinks into my cells. I absorb it, and wonder if he feels my fear too.

That first night, right after the incident, the verse my parents taught me reassured me. I believed it, but the longer we've gone with no leads, with no idea who was behind that stunt in the parking lot, the fainter that truth becomes. Since we arrived in Vegas, it has offered me little assurance. I don't know if love actually does cast out fear, but I know I'll do anything to preserve our future. If I didn't know it before, the moment I thought that fan was a threat, it became real to me.

I cup his face between my hands, forcing his eyes to mine.

"I would do anything for you." I inch up on my toes so my lips brush against his when I speak. "I wouldn't even pause if I had to die for you, Rhyson."

"No." He clips it out, squeezing his eyes shut and rolling his forehead in a slow denial against mine. "Don't say that. Baby, don't ever say that. I couldn't stay here without you."

Tears rise in my throat. We haven't talked much more about the shirt, about what it means, about someone being unhappy enough with our engagement they'd do something so awful. About what else they could try or be capable of. We dove into this showcase, probably as much to distract ourselves from the incident as to prepare for the event. It's only now that I grasp how heavily it has weighed on both our minds. How we've both considered the sacrifices we'd make for the other if it came to that.

"You'd die for me wouldn't you, Rhyson?" I whisper.

"Twice if I could," he responds without hesitation, voice husky and eyes burning a hole through the last of my control.

I strain up, locking my elbows around his neck. He swoops in, delving into my mouth and palming the back of my head, crushing passion between our lips like a ripe fruit that bursts, that pops, and we sip its juices from one another. And all the things we haven't said, the fears and the uncertainty, flow from me to him, from him to me, in a wordless dialogue of lips and tongue and teeth. He kneads my breast through my dress. He licks down my neck, his mouth open, hot and wet over my breast through the thin linen.

"Get this off." His guttural words rumble against my nipple. "Get it fucking off."

My fingers fumble with the little button at my neck he helped me with in the elevator hours ago. We've been building this fire ever since then—every touch, every breath. Even seeing Dub only poured gasoline on something simmering between us all day. The top finally falls to my waist, slumping around my hips, and I bare myself for him. He squats to draw one nipple into the hot cavern of his mouth while he squeezes and rolls the other.

He drops to his knees, reaches under my dress and rolls my

panties over my legs and to my feet. I step out eagerly, already damp with anticipation. He pulls one leg over his shoulder and disappears beneath the hem of my dress. He knows where I want his mouth. I'm dripping for him. Begging for him, but he kisses inside my thigh, slowing to suck and lick, drawing on the flesh with such strength I know he's marking me. It's an eternity before his fingers spread me, forever before he sucks the button of flesh nestled there. He draws the lips into his mouth, groaning and gripping my butt, pressing me deeper into his hunger. Consumed, he sups between my legs. I slap one hand against the slick surface of the refrigerator behind me. The other grips his shoulder for balance, for purchase, for an anchor in the riptide. A kaleidoscope of sensations explodes through me, fanning out from my core and quaking through my heart.

"Rhys!" The orgasm demands his name from me on a sob. "Baby, yes. Please . . . sweet Jesus . . . please."

I don't think I've ever come so hard, so fast, but I'm like a keg primed to blow. It's not even the physical touch of him in the most secret, vulnerable places of my body. It's the way we touch one another in the secret, most vulnerable places of our souls. I grind against his mouth as I come down, limp and barely upright. His head emerges from beneath my dress, the dark hair rumpled and bronze-streaked. His lips glisten. He traces the words tattooed over my ribcage, his eyes and fingers venerate, worshipful.

"I love . . . I need . . ." The muscles of his throat work around the emotion darkening his eyes. He doesn't have to say another word. I'm hollow inside without him. I need it too, tunneling my fingers into his hair and nodding frantically.

He lifts me at my waist, holding me above him, carrying me, kissing me, walking swiftly to the dining room table and shoving the elaborate centerpiece aside. He lays me out and crawls over me. I wiggle my way out of the dress altogether until my naked back and bottom touch the table's cool mahogany wood. Eyes never leaving mine, he sheds his clothes, until he's as naked as I am. My fingers burn with the need to trace the notes and lyrics decorating his lean chest. Smooth, golden skin stretches taut over the muscles of his arms and shoulders. His breaths grow heavier with every second, contracting the tightly stacked abdominal muscles. I reach between us and grab his cock. It pulses hot and hard in my fingers. My lips wrap around his nipple, and I suck and pull. Suck and pull. Suck and pull until he's groaning, eyes shut tight from the sensual torture.

"Pep!" His voice booms in the quiet suite. "Dammit, yes."

He shackles my wrists in one hand over my head, pressing one of my legs back, cracking me open. I hook the other leg over his hip, and he raids my body. The first thrust is so rough and deep the air expels from my chest, but I urge him on, pull him in closer. I can't get him deep enough. I need him thrusting into my soul.

"More." I refuse to let his eyes go. "It's all yours, Rhyson."

Whispering "fuck yes" into the hair fanning around my head and shoulders, he releases my wrists and hooks an arm under my knee. The cadence his body sets is bruising, frenetic, scooting me inches up the table every time he pulls back and plunges forward like a battering ram. I dig my heels into his ass, urging him deeper and deeper and harder and faster; begging him to rush past my limits and over my borders. I meet every thrust. We give and take, our hips engaged in a salacious call and response. I arch up my chest for him to ravage my nipples, sending him back and forth between them, one breast and the other, biting and licking and suckling unrelentingly. My breasts are so swollen and red and deliciously tender, even his breath panting over them pulls a trigger in me. A scream rends me in half, and my love and desperation and fear—they gush out all over him. He pounds into me, frenzied, bellowing, head flung back, neck strained with the release. And his love pours into me. Hot and liquid, it fills me.

He slows until he's still. Our breath breaches the tiny space separating our lips. I inhale the smell of our bodies tangled. My essence and his, mingled. The scent of our souls communing, a plume of sweet smoke, is an opiate to the senses that intoxicates me. I'm high on us together.

He caresses my face, fingertips following the line of my eyebrows, my cheekbone, my lips. All the while, his eyes plumb mine, searching and finding the epicenter of this storm. We are both shaken, emotion trembling through our muscles and fusing our gaze. There's nothing else in this world I want to see.

"Marry me," he says hoarsely, propped on one hand, his stomach and thighs taut and tensed above me.

I blink up at him. Thrown and dazed and still lightheaded. I cup his chin and find a way, even in this torrent of emotion, to smile.

"I am." I wiggle the finger weighted with my engagement ring.

He gives a swift shake of his head, his face set in familiar determined lines.

"No, tonight. Marry me tonight. I don't want to wait."

"Rhys, you don't have to—"

"I have to. I want to." He takes my lips sweetly, whispering against them. "Don't make me wait. We're in Vegas, the only place it can happen tonight."

"Is this about Dub?"

He narrows his eyes and tenses into stone.

"You really think I'd let him dictate anything in our life?"

"No, but you have to admit the timing is odd." I reach up to caress his jaw, wanting to loosen the tension Dub's name introduced.

"I told you before I didn't want to wait, Pep."

"But I-I, well, I thought you wanted the ceremony," I stutter. "The dress. Our family and friends. Our . . . all of it."

"I do want all of that, and we'll have it. Later. But the marriage, I want that to start tonight." He feathers kisses over my face and down my neck. His mouth is a persuasion. His heart hammering into mine, an offer I can't refuse. "Baby, say yes."

"But, Rhys, if we—"

"I won't be any more certain in a few months than I am right now. Than I am tonight," he says. "We'll work everything out later. All the plans and the schedules and the details. It'll happen. I'll give you the wedding of your dreams. I promise. But tonight, let's just jump."

He tips my chin up, eyes imploring.

"Leap for me, Kai."

Everything heavy—the fear that has hung over me like a cloud since that night in the parking lot, the panic today thinking someone wanted to hurt him, everything that would hold me back, falls away at the love in his eyes. At the promise sketched in every line of his face. A smile, so wide and so irrepressibly sure, fights its way through the emotion swelling in my chest and settles on my face. And I don't think before I speak.

I just leap.

"Yes."

15

Rhyson

"YOU ARE ONE CRAZY ASS MOTHERFUCKER."

Not exactly the words you want to hear from your would-be best man before the wedding. I scowl at Marlon lounging on the cream-colored leather couch in my suite.

"That's all you have to say?" I take a sip of the bottled water from the refrigerator. Just thinking about what happened in that kitchen a few hours ago has me wanting to fast forward through this ceremony and to start the honeymoon. Not that we get an actual honeymoon yet. Maybe we should have done one of those drive-thru weddings.

"Dude, you call me an hour ago and say you're getting married tonight? In Vegas." Marlon chuckles and shakes his head, setting the locs around his shoulders into motion. "It's crazy."

It may sound crazy, but I know it's right. In the corridor earlier and then when Kai and I made love on the dining room table, everything crystallized for me. I knew it. I've known it. Kai didn't take me seriously when I told her I didn't want to wait. This would have happened sooner or later. There's no way I'd wait to plan the elaborate ceremony we discussed. Marrying Kai is like a mandate in my heart. We'll have the flowers and the perfect setting and all our family and the whole shebang. I want it too. But more than all of that, I want Kai as my wife, in every way that counts. And I want it tonight.

"If you think it's so crazy," I tell Marlon curtly, "You don't have to be here."

"It is crazy." Marlon flashes a grin. "But then you've been crazy about this girl from the beginning. I've never seen you this way about anyone. About anything. Why would I expect your wedding to be any less crazy?"

His smile fades and his expression loses most of its humor.

"And I wouldn't miss it for the world."

We've been together through every stage of our lives for the last decade or so. The ride I'm on wouldn't have been the same without him. My circle has always been tight, and almost from the beginning he's been closer than anyone else.

"Marlon, man, that means a lot. There's nobody else I'd have standing with me." We man-hug fast before things get any heavier. "Glad you're here for it."

I break up the moment by walking over to the desk drawer and retrieving the marriage license. Getting married in Vegas is easier than getting your driver's license, but you still have to appear in person before a Clark County marriage clerk. That whole "in person" thing was a small hurdle. Ella helped pull together some light disguising for us, and Gep was the only person we took with us to the clerk's office. There was no line and only a few people milling about and minding their own business. None of them recognized us. Bristol found one of those wedding packages where the officiant comes to you. She'll probably line his pockets to ensure he delays filing the documentation as long as legally possible. That should give us ten days before our marriage becomes public record.

It's been a whirlwind of loose ends and details, but I think we've checked all the boxes. The biggest box was Aunt Ruthie. She wasn't happy with us when we called to tell her our plan, but she was happy for us. She's on the other side of the country and can't drop everything and get to Vegas in time, but we promised her we'll do it big soon. Kai had to leave a voice mail for San, who's back in Turks and Caicos on assignment. I'm glad she's going ahead with the wedding tonight even though the two people who are like family aren't here. I felt a moment of remorse, but it passed. I'm too thrilled that this is happening tonight. As much as I wish Aunt Ruthie and San were here, as glad as I am that my friends can be, tonight—it's for us, for Kai and me.

Ella comes from down the hall, smiling.

"She's almost ready." Her expert eye runs over me from head to toe.

"What?" I glance over the dark suit I bought an hour ago. I even have on a tie, the equivalent of wearing a unicorn around my neck it's so rare. The tailor did wonders on such short notice. "This is Armani. You don't approve?"

"You look very handsome." Ella plucks a white rose from the vase on a side table, snapping the stem and slipping it into the lapel button hole. "Nice touch, huh?"

I murmur a "thanks" and burrow my hands deep into my pockets. My heart hammers my rib cage. My palms are sweating. Now I'm pacing. I rake my fingers through the hair I just combed. I don't care. Kai's seen my hair a mess.

"Where the hell is Bristol?" I clip the question out. I'm dialing her when the suite door opens, and she steps in waving her key card.

"It's just me." She gestures behind her. "And Reverend Mason. We were lucky to find him."

Kai insisted the wedding be officiated by a minister. I guess that's her Baptist upbringing kicking in. Shrek could perform the ceremony as far as I care, as long as it's legal and binding.

"Hi." I step forward to shake the reverend's hand. "Thank you for coming on such short notice."

"No problem, Mr. Gray." Reverend Mason's face reddens a little. "My daughter is a huge fan, by the way."

"Um, you know you can't mention this to her, right?" I try to keep my voice even and friendly. "Did Bristol talk with you about—"

"Reverend Mason has already signed the NDA. We've gone over everything, Rhys," Bristol interrupts. "We can trust him to be discreet."

"Thanks." I relax my expression into a smile for the reverend. "I'd be happy to sign something or give your daughter anything you think she'd like. If you could just wait until later to give it to her."

"I'll handle all of that." Bristol brushes her fingers over my by-now-unruly hair. "Ella, can't we do something with this?"

"I don't give a damn about . . ." I catch the reverend's eye and grimace. You'd think being around Aunt Ruthie would curb my profanity reflex, but my tongue is as unruly as my hair. "Forget about my hair. Can we just do this?"

"Before we do," Bristol says. "I need to speak to you and Kai privately."

Impatience draws a quick breath through my nostrils and tightens my lips.

"Bris, can't it wait?"

"No. It'll be quick."

I motion for her to follow me down the hall toward the suite's master bedroom. Even though it's my bedroom, I knock. Who knows what kind of bridal shit Kai's doing in there?

"Come in." She sounds . . . nervous? I guess I am too.

"Hey, babe. Bristol needs to—"

I stop at the threshold, and the words dry up in my mouth. Maybe the words actually fall out since my mouth is hanging open. Kai looks . . . I can't imagine she'll be any more beautiful when we do the fancy ceremony for everyone else than she does right now. At least not to me. An ivory dress nips at her narrow waist and sheathes her curves, falling to mid-calf. The dress shimmers with something that looks like gold dust. I know it can't be, but that's how it looks to me. Like she's been gilded. Ella piled all of her hair up, and even wove a few golden threads into the dark strands. The dress is strapless, displaying the sweet curves of her shoulders and the elegant line of her collarbone. Her only jewelry is gold studs in her ears, the nameplate necklace I gave her last Christmas, her grandmother's gold chain, and the sapphire I put on her finger not even two weeks ago. She's wearing more make-up than usual, but it's just right. I need to buy Ella something outrageous to thank her for the job she's done.

"Rhyson." Kai gives me a half-exasperated glance. "I know this isn't a traditional wedding, but it's still bad luck for you to be in here."

"Fuck luck." I step forward and close my hands around her waist, drawing her into me. "You look . . . God, I can't even put it into words."

"Oh, this old thing." She leans into my chest and smiles up at me. "There's this great vintage shop a couple blocks up. I wouldn't be me if my wedding dress wasn't older than I am. Well, at least my first wedding dress. Ella saw it and thought it was very Doris Day in That Touch of Mink."

"I have no idea what that means, but you look perfect." I lay my nose to the spot behind her ear, inhaling the scent of pears and cinnamon. "And I promise we'll do something elaborate and over the top later for your second wedding. Thank you for marrying me tonight."

"Thank you for asking." She runs her nose along the line of my jaw.

"I hate to break this up, but we need to chat before the ceremony." Bristol's eyes soften when they rest on Kai. "You're a beautiful bride."

"Thanks, Bris." Kai smiles warmly and looks between the two of us. "What's up?"

Bristol clears her throat. Again, that always means she's about to say something she knows I don't want to hear. It may as well be a battle cry because it always ends with us brawling.

"We just need to sign some paperwork before the ceremony."

"What kind of paperwork?" I stare at my sister, who is all of a sudden preoccupied with the clasp on her bag and avoiding my eyes.

"Um, well your lawyer sent over an, um . . ." Bristol doesn't finish the sentence. She just thrusts the small stack of papers at us. Neither Kai nor I make a move to take them.

"Bristol, that better not be a pre-nup." I keep my voice low, but anger pounds the blood in my ears.

"Rhyson, just hear me out. I—"

"Dammit, Bris!" My fingers drive into my hair, landing on the back of my neck where pressure builds "Why would you do this?"

"Rhys, it's okay," Kai says softly.

"The hell it is." I look down at her, the purity of her face, her sweetness, making me feel even worse about this ugliness marring what was supposed to be perfect. "Do you think I need a piece of paper to protect me? From you?"

"No, I don't think that." Kai's eyes drift from my face to my sister's. "I don't think Bristol actually believes that either."

"I don't. I trust you, Kai." Bristol grimaces. "I mean, now I do. When we first met, I wasn't sure what to make of you. I know you love my brother, but my job is to protect him from anything that could ever go wrong, to be prepared for any and everything. I had to contact your lawyer, Rhyson, to let him know this was happening."

"You had to?" A bitter laugh chafes my throat. "If you think she's signing—"

"Give it to me." Kai extends her hand for the papers. "I don't care."

"You will not sign a damn pre-nup, Pep." I gently press her arm back to her side. "It's worthless if you sign it and I don't, and there's no way in hell I'm signing it. I'll rip it in half as soon as I get my hands on it."

"It doesn't matter." Kai clutches both my hands between hers against her chest. "You have a lot of stuff, Rhyson. And your team is just looking out for you. I'd be shocked if they hadn't suggested it. You and I know. We know that the only thing I want is every day with you for the rest of my life. I don't need anything else."

Tears glimmer in her eyes, and her mouth trembles.

"You, baby. Not your money. You know that, and I don't care what anyone else thinks."

"Which is exactly why we're not signing it." I cup her chin and pass my thumb over her cheek. "If you divorce me, don't love me anymore, leave me, the last thing I'll care about is how much of my money you take with you when you go. A life without you would be a lot worse than losing half my stuff."

The sound of ripping paper tears my attention away from Kai.

"Oh, fuck it," Bristol says. "At least I can tell him I tried."

I smile at my twin sister holding two halves of the pre-nup.

"There's a tender heart under all that bitch, Bristol." I take Kai's hand and lead her toward the door.

"Don't tell anybody, especially not your lawyer. I have a rep to maintain." Bristol rolls her eyes. "Come on. Let's get married."

When we re-enter the suite, two lines of votive candles form an aisle of sorts down the center of the spacious living room. Ella must have plucked all the flower arrangements in the room to pad the carpet with a trail of rose petals leading to Reverend Mason waiting with his Bible. Bristol goes to stand beside Marlon, looking straight ahead and blinking furiously. Ella already clutches her Kleenex, sniffing before we've even started.

Kai and I hold hands and walk down the carpeted makeshift aisle pelted with flowers. The light from the candles makes the gold threads in Kai's dress shine even brighter. I can't take my eyes off her, and I can't believe this is happening.

"We are gathered here today in the sight of God . . ."

Reverend Mason's words barely penetrate my consciousness. My mind doesn't wander, but deliberately reaches back to the first time I saw Kai in Grady's music room. From that first look, she planted a hook in my heart, and she's been reeling me in ever since. I think my heart would collapse without it now. That hook somehow holds my heart together.

"Love is patient and kind, never jealous or envious, never boastful or proud. Love is never haughty or selfish or rude. Love does not demand its own way. Love does not hold grudges," Reverend Mason reads. "If you love someone, you will be loyal to them no matter what the costs. You will always believe in them, always expect the best in them, and will always stand your ground in defending them."

I know it's a verse from the Bible, but I'm not sure which one. Kai has probably known it by heart since she was a kid. I may not know it, but it perfectly sums up what we've been through, and how our love has survived. I want the chance to show Kai I'll be loyal no matter the cost. That I'll always believe in her and expect the best. That even with some kook out there possibly wanting her dead, I'll stand my ground defending her till the end.

"Do you have anything you'd like to say?" Reverend Mason asks. "Any personal vows prepared?"

Kai shakes her head no, but I take her chin between my fingers and speak the vows I wrote for her long before this day arrived.

I was lost before you found me, or maybe I found you
Maybe it was fate or kismet, or something much more true
It could have been an answered prayer, a sacred certainty
All I know is what we have now. I've got no plans to leave
Not an ocean, not forever
Nothing wide or deep
Will ever end this love between us
My soul is yours to keep

Tears stand in her eyes for a few seconds before they spill over, splashing her cheeks with the emotion that reverberates between us like a sound wave. After a moment, she sniffs and echoes the vow from our song back to me, her voice strong and sweet. The silence following her words feels almost holy; like a prayer and a promise wed.

"Rhyson Gray, do you take Kai Anne Pearson, to be your lawfully wedded wife?" Reverend Mason asks.

A huge, hot lump fills my throat, and I barely squeeze the words past it.

"I do."

"Do you promise to love, honor, cherish, and protect her, forsaking all others and holding only unto her forevermore?"

"I do."

"Kai Anne Pearson, do you take Rhyson Gray to be your lawfully wedded husband?" Reverend Mason asks.

Even knowing she accepted my proposal, wears my ring, and stands here with a white dress and witnesses, I hold my breath. Surely it's an open secret that I'm not good enough for this girl. That I don't deserve even a day with her, much less the rest of my life. But do I care? Hell, no. She may be too good for me, but I'm marrying her before she comes to her senses. I've considered her mine almost as long as I've known her. And when she says those two words, they'll place a seal over our hearts.

"I do."

With a satisfied smile, Reverend Mason says the words I wasn't prepared for.

"May we have the rings?"

"Shit," I hiss under my breath. Maybe not far enough under enough because the reverend's eyebrows climb his forehead with surprise and possible disapproval.

"I didn't uh . . ." I squeeze Kai's fingers between mine. "I already have the wedding band that goes with your ring, baby. With everything being last minute, I just didn't think. It's in LA."

"We'll improvise," Ella says, stepping forward and carefully extracting one of the golden threads from Kai's hair.

She tears the thread with her teeth and offers each of us half. Kai ties her golden thread around my left ring finger. I do the same for her, nudging her engagement ring up so I can tie my gold thread around her finger. It disappears under the thick platinum band immediately, but I don't care. I know it's there.

"By the power vested in me by the state of Nevada," Reverend Mason says. "I now pronounce you man and wife. You may kiss the bride."

I look down at Kai, so impossibly beautiful. So completely mine. It's fitting that there's no veil to lift. We disposed of those long ago. Nothing hides her from me. And nothing hides me from her. We are open. We are known. We are one. We are married.

We kiss.

16

Kai

I WOKE UP THIS MORNING AS the only actual Mrs. Rhyson Gray in the world.

Not just wearing the t-shirt. Not just the name I may or may not have scribbled on notebooks and other random surfaces in the past like a lovesick teenager. Not some fantasy I awake from only to find reality so much less.

I woke up Mrs. Rhyson Gray, and it is officially the best day of my life.

It wasn't the first time I woke up in his arms. It wasn't even the first time I woke to find him leaned up on an elbow, hair tousled, and his silvery eyes contemplating me, hungry and demanding before the sun was even up. All those things have happened before. But cementing forever yesterday with our wedding ceremony, assuring that all those things will happen for the rest of our lives, that forged something deeper and richer than I thought possible. I know he feels it too. In the morning light, he answered every kiss with wonder. Every touch, with awe. Every moment we bared ourselves to one another felt like a miracle.

And this joy.

Oh, God, this joy is the strongest element on earth. It's titanium. It is the most fragile thing I've ever held. It's gossamer. It infused every look we shared over breakfast in bed. Locked behind our closed suite door, it drowned out the noise of our fears and uncertainties. It has even electrified my performance.

I haven't been on stage in weeks, and I've missed it, but it's never been like this. The connection with the audience even seems tinged with this joy. I'm doing what I was created to do with the man I was made to love. I know there is more ahead. I have no doubt when I give birth to our baby in a few months, it will even surpass this feeling. But today, still aching from his love this morning, wearing a gold string under my engagement ring to remind me we'll have this for the rest of our lives, and performing before a packed house like a woman possessed, this day is pinnacle. It is zenith.

"How You Like It," my duet with Grip from his upcoming album, set this crowd ablaze. An electric current has zipped through the hotel's amphitheater since the opening act. The more people experience Kilimanjaro, the more they're astounded and impressed by their talent the way Rhyson and I were that first time we heard them at the beach festival. Luke solidified what America knew when they voted for him on Total Package last season. He's a formidable artist with huge commercial appeal and the talent to back it up. And Grip. Just wow. Grip is so laidback sometimes it's easy to forget that in his heart, he's a poet. That in his soul, he's an activist. That in his mind lies true brilliance. His lyrics remind us. He's magnetic onstage, drawing the crowd to him, luring them with his charisma, and then with his talent, feeding them from the palm of his hand.

It was easy to think of this as just a Vegas show, but Bristol outdid herself. Cameras from every media outlet imaginable line the perimeter of the theater. The showcase is streaming online, and millions of people are seeing the juggernaut Rhyson has assembled to launch Prodigy. It's eclectic, each act so different from the other, but so excellent in its own right. Rhyson has put together something special, and I'm so proud of him as he joins Grip and me onstage when our song ends.

He asks Grip a few questions, and their easy rapport and obvious friendship endears the audience to them both even more. As planned, Grip leaves me onstage with Rhyson to segue into a brief interview before he closes the show.

"So, Kai." The intimacy of Rhyson's eyes on me whispers a secret in front of the whole world. "Now I'm supposed to ask you a few questions."

I nod, a little nervous, but prepared. Bristol sent me the questions beforehand, and they're pretty standard. What's not standard is having your husband, who everyone thinks is your fiancé, who is one of the biggest rock stars in the world . . . and also the father of your super secret baby . . . ask you said questions.

"We had these prepared." Rhyson holds up an index card for everyone to see. "But I just thought, what's the fun in that?"

He tosses the card, and most of my composure, over his shoulder. Wicked glee infuses the smirk he levels at me.

"Let's go off-road a little."

The crowd laughs and cheers, probably because my face shows my shock and apprehension.

"So, Kai." Rhyson puts on his "I'm going to be serious, no, really, I am" face. "Can you tell us why your hummus always tastes like butt?"

The audience explodes laughing. I can't help it. I give him the evilest eye I can muster before I break down, covering my warm face and laughing through my fingers.

"Okay. Real question this time," he says. "Tell us the one artist who's inspired you the most."

He already knows this, of course.

"I'd have to say Cher." I'm braced for his teasing, but despite the knowing glint in his eyes, it never comes, so I continue. "I love her stage presence. Love what a complete entertainer she is. Whether she was singing, dancing, cutting up on a variety show, or winning Oscars and Emmys for her acting, she's always excellent and undeniably talented. And her work ethic is amazing."

I force myself to stop gushing because I could go on all day about Cher, and I don't want to hear about it from him later.

His next few questions are a great mix of serious and outrageous. I find myself relaxing and feeling more comfortable talking than I ever have. I love the music, but I'm not actually an extrovert, so sometimes I feel stiff or less than sparkly in interviews. I realize that Rhyson recognized that and tailored the questions to bring out some of the things only those closest to me ever get to see or know. He tailored the questions to the things he loves about me, and it makes the audience like me more. I can feel their perception of me shifting as Rhyson guides them to the conclusion he reached long ago.

I'm pretty awesome.

At least in his mind. And I sense, now, a little more in theirs.

"Last question." He smiles, but something hides behind the humor in his eyes. "You ready?"

"Bring it on." I smile out at the crowd.

"What was the greatest moment of your life?"

My smile slowly fades as I seriously consider his question. I'm standing here, literally performing in front of more people than I ever thought I would. I always used to dream of performing for my father, and though I can't pick him out of this crowd of faces, he's here somewhere with the sister I'll meet for the first time after the show. As bitter as my relationship with him has been, there's still something sweet there for me to savor. I'm married to a man whose voice comforted me in my darkest days and who ushered me out of grief and darkness into light with his friendship and love. I'm carrying his child, and every day, I'm overwhelmed by his devotion. Tears sting my eyes and burn my throat. I'm humbled by it. Gratitude, unconditional love, and, yes, joy rise and rise, levitating me from the inside like helium.

"Kai, your greatest moment?" Rhyson prompts, his eyes so full of undeniable affection.

"This one," I whisper with a teary smile.

He surprises everyone, me most of all, by slipping an arm around my waist, cupping my neck, and kissing me so sweetly on the lips. I can't help it. Even with millions watching, love and hunger push me up on my toes to get closer to him. To get more of him. The pieces none of these people will ever have, will ever know. He groans into the kiss without deepening it. We both know if we open our mouths just the tiniest bit and get a taste, if there is even a glimpse of tongue, it's going viral.

The whoops and cheering are still going after he releases me and I make my way backstage. Grip high fives me and Luke makes kissy faces. The Kilimanjaro guys, who I'm still getting to know, just give me "awwwws" and eye rolls. One of them even sings "Rhyson and Kai, sitting in a tree, k-i-s-s-i-n-g." I'm like a cheerleader trapped in a fraternity with these guys. I need to find at least one other girl for the Prodigy family.

Rhyson's onstage, talking about his vision for the label and all the exciting things developing this year.

"He didn't mention your album." Grip looks down at me, arms folded over his broad chest and a question stamped on his face.

I bite my lip under Grip's scrutiny. Rhyson hasn't talked about the revised schedule, of course, with anyone since no one else knows about the baby. I don't know if it was the wedding. Maybe it was yesterday's scare with the fan, though unfounded, that has put everything into perspective, but as much as it stings, I've made peace with the delay. Rhyson is too much of a perfectionist to rush the process. The entire process. And momentum is broken if I'm having a baby in a few months. It hurts. I'm disappointed, but nothing can dent this joy.

"I guess he's reassessing." I shrug. "Probably a timing issue. It's fine."

"Well, dude knows what he's doing." Grip grins. "Best friend or not, I wouldn't have signed with him if I didn't believe that."

Rhyson's instincts are impeccable. Every artist signed to Prodigy believes that. Believes in him. After all the resistance I put up to signing with him initially, I'm now the biggest believer of all. I watch my husband charming a million people with a single smile and have to smile myself. A believer? Who am I kidding? When it comes to Rhyson, I'm a fanatic.

"Who's that with Bristol?" The undercurrent darkening Grip's voice forces my eyes past Rhyson, backstage left. We can see Bristol across from us in the wings on the opposite side of the stage. A man, tall and blonde, wearing a suit that looks like it's lined with money, rests one hand on Bristol's hip, and his head dips a few inches so he can whisper in her ear. Bristol looks more relaxed than I've seen her in weeks, her smile wide and her eyes flirting. It could be because the showcase, which has consumed her more than any of us, is almost over. Or it could be because one of the country's most eligible bachelors has his hands all over her.

"Um, well." I fold my lips in, being careful with my words. Who doesn't know how Grip feels about Bristol? Maybe I'm the only one who suspects Bristol feels something, too, but you wouldn't know that looking at her now.

"'Um, well' isn't an answer, Kai." Grip's eyes don't waver from the couple who look so perfect together, both tall, his fair coloring a dramatic contrast to Bristol's dark hair. "Who the hell is that dude?"

"Charles Parker." I loop my elbow through Grip's, feeling the tension cording his arm. "His family owns the Parker Group and all the Park Hotels, including this one."

"And half the world with it." Worry creases Grips forehead. "Am I fooling myself? Maybe she doesn't . . ."

I elbow him in the ribs.

"Hey, look at me," I urge when he can't seem to stop watching them. Jealousy lives in the dark eyes he finally turns to me. "She does."

His expression eases by degrees, and one corner of his firm lips quirks, looking more like the Grip I'm used to seeing.

"I used to believe that, but now I'm not so sure."

"When did you believe that?" He doesn't answer, but drops a guard over his expression. "When, Grip?"

"It was a long time ago," he answers softly, eyes drifting back to Parker and Bristol. "Maybe too long ago."

"Well, most guys who like a girl find every possible way to be around them." I notice Rhyson sitting down at the piano to close out the show. "He did."

"You're right about that. I've never seen Rhys that persistent about anything but music." His grin goes as quickly as it came, giving way to the considering look he gives me. "You mean I should let her be my manager? I just don't want to be her job."

"Grip, I hate to break it to you, but you're already her job. Anything associated with Prodigy is her job. It's up to you to take advantage of that." I place a finger over my lips. "Now hush. My husband's about to play."

He squeezes me into a side hug, and then we both go quiet while we wait for Rhyson to begin.

And we wait.

It's too quiet for too long before I remember, before I notice him massaging his right hand. With everything that has happened over the last day, I'd forgotten about his hand. I know he hears the difference, and I know what he means, but this crowd won't. He's still the best musician I've ever heard. I will him to look up from the keys, to seek me out like he always does. Finally, he searches the shadows until he finds me. I don't wait for him to signal me. This time I signal him.

I tug my ear and press my hand to my heart.

"I live you," I mouth to him, hoping my eyes tell him all the things I would say if he were close enough. That he's rare. That he's the gift, not the talent of his hands. That even if he could never play another note, he'd still have me, and I'd adore him no less.

Just as the crowd starts to murmur, growing uncertain about the delay, Rhyson smiles, rubs the tiny gold thread tied around his ring finger and begins to play. Not with just his hands, but pouring his whole body into it. Like the first time I ever saw him in Grady's music room, passion wreaths his face until he's lost to the intimacy of him and his instrument. His fingers run nimbly from one end of the piano to the other, shoulders heaving with the effort of coaxing sounds from another realm into this one. It's not a song from a previous album. Not a song anyone has ever played on the radio. Not a tune I've heard drifting up from the music room. It's classical, but his original. The gentle swells surrender to monstrous crescendos. This music crests and crashes over everyone listening and holds us rapt. It towers over anything even I've ever heard him play. From measure to measure, the song evolves like a living thing, at once timid and next terrifying with black keys and dark notes, and finally with tender breath. So subtle, each note like a whisper that finally, when I'm not sure I can withstand another moment, dies.

When I was a little girl, my father always talked about a great cloud of witnesses in Heaven. Those who have gone before and wait for us beyond. He used to tell me they're always there observing this life, but every once in a while, something so glorious happens on earth, they find a way to join in. And I imagine I hear their applause because the response is so thunderous in the amphitheater, surely we aren't the only ones clapping, yelling, asking for more.

Instead of giving us more, Rhyson looks around almost like he'd forgotten we were there. He pushes away from the piano, shaking himself a little, and waves to the artists in the wings, encouraging us to join him onstage. I would never have had this with Malcolm—this energy and sense of family surging through our little group as we link arms. It feels so good to be tucked into Rhyson as he reminds everyone that the night is about us and the future of Prodigy.

We start to exit, leaving Rhyson to wrap up the last few things

Bristol needed covered. I don't know why I look out at the audience as we leave the stage. Maybe to check just in case I do, by some miracle, spot my father and half-sister. Whatever compels me to look out, I'll always be grateful.

I don't see my father, but I see those blue eyes boiling with resentment. Narrowed with an inexplicable indignation. Only this time they're not fixed on me. Those eyes fix on my husband with a rage so cold, I shiver. The other artists keep walking, brushing past me as they return to the wings. I stop where I am and will her to turn those eyes on me. I silently, recklessly beg her to direct that wrath at me, but she doesn't. Slowly like she's got all the time in the world, she raises her arm and aims a gun at the love of my life.

Those immediately around her react, shrieking and climbing over other people to scurry away. It all unfolds in slow motion, and yet in an instant. In the space of a blink. In the span of a breath. The commotion draws Rhyson's attention, but he doesn't know. He has no idea, and by the time he processes what's happening, it will be too late.

Would you die for me, Rhyson?

Twice if I could.

You will always believe in them, always expect the best in them, and will always stand your ground in defending them. Till death do us part.

Perfect love casts out fear.

Leap for me, Kai.

Leap!

And before my mind can talk my heart out of it, I do.

17

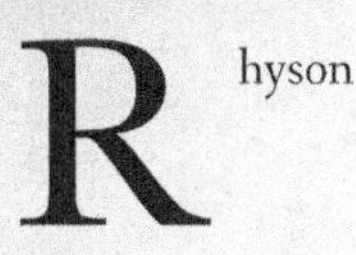hyson

SHE'S IN MY ARMS.

Like so many mornings when we wake up, Kai is in my arms. And for a fraction of a second, I find comfort in that like I always do, but then reality rushes in, tidal in its ferocity. We're on the stage floor, not in the bed where, with lazy whispers and ardent touches, we share our dreams and hopes and fears. Where we share our love. The world around me is made of mayhem and hysteria, and high-pitched screams pierce the dense fog in my head.

One minute I'm relieved with how well I played, watching everyone walk offstage, and the next Kai is flinging herself in front of me. We're on the floor, arms and legs twisted around each other.

"Kai!" Her name torpedoes out of me.

I sit up, cradling her in my arms. Her face is blanched of all color, and her head flops back lifelessly. Dark red blooms from her back, spreading like a virus over the pristine pink of her dress, discoloring my jeans and seeping into my skin. The blood evacuates fast and heavy like it's being chased from her body. I can't tell where it's coming from, but it's everywhere. It spills into a sea around us, and every ounce drains her life, takes her a little farther away from me.

"Rhys." My name passes like a puff of smoke past her lips. Her eyelids flutter and roll back in her head.

"Kai, dammit." My voice wobbles and I push the hair back from her face. "What were you thinking? I told you . . . you shouldn't have . . ."

My words die when she finds my hand, her grip weak.

"I wasn't thinking." Her breaths come more labored and choppy. "I just . . ."

Tears trail from her eyes and puddle in her ears.

"Our baby," she whispers. "Oh, God, Rhyson. Our baby. I'm so sorry."

"No." I press my forehead to hers, our tears mingling on her cold cheeks. "You're gonna be okay. You'll be okay. Just . . ."

It hurts to swallow. It hurts to breathe. It hurts to be perfectly fine when she is in pain and slipping away . . . because of me.

"Just stay with me." I press my lips to her hair. "Please just . . ."

Kai's eyes flicker until they close, and blood trickles from one corner of her mouth. Needles of panic sting every limb, injecting me with poison and fear. Pain overwhelms me, sudden and thorough, leaving no part of me untouched. Leaving me numb. I can't move any more than she can.

"Rhyson." Bristol rushes over to us onstage, her eyes darting from Kai's ashen face to mine, her eyes wide and afraid. "Is she . . . Oh, God. We called nine-one-one."

With visibly trembling fingers, Bristol pushes her hair back.

"The paramedics should be here soon." She gulps, her lips pressing into a straight line. "They said we should staunch the bleeding. Use your shirt."

I rip my shirt over my head and search for the source of the blood gurgling from Kai's back. The shirt quickly becomes red and soaked by the steady, heavy stream.

"Where the hell are they?" I mean to growl the words, but they come out weak. Desperate. Helpless and terrified.

"On their way. They should be close." Bristol presses her hand on top of mine to add more pressure. "She's gonna be okay, Rhyson."

"If she . . . I can't . . ." I shake my head and clutch Kai closer. "I can't lose her, Bris."

"You won't." Bristol's eyes latch onto something over my shoulder, her expression collapsing with relief. "Over here! She's over here!"

Two paramedics rush onstage with a stretcher. They load Kai quickly and start rolling her back out.

"Desert Springs," one of them yells back. "If you need to follow."

I shake off my shock and run after them.

"I'm her husband. I'm riding with her."

"We'll meet you there," Bristol says, her voice stretched thin with fright and stress.

Even as quickly as they're rolling the gurney, I manage to grab Kai's hand and keep pace with them. I have to touch her, but as soon as we climb up into the back of the ambulance, they urge me back and away from her. It's only as my bare back hits the cold ambulance wall that I remember I stripped off my shirt. It lays disregarded, a crimson bundle on the floor.

"Blood pressure's falling," one of them says. "Breathing's not good."

"Her lips are turning blue. Why are her lips turning blue?" I can't believe that's my voice, urgent and demanding. I don't feel demanding. I feel helpless like I have no rights to anything. Certainly not to the rest of my life with Kai.

"Too much blood. Where's she hit?" the other asks, not of me, but of the other paramedic. "Let's get this off."

He cuts Kai's tiny pink dress right up the middle. I'm not prepared for all the blood. If I focus on it too much, on seeing my girl like this, I'll lose my mind. My brain fixates on useless information and minutiae to create a safer space for me. Like how tragedy has a way of stripping us of our privacy and our dignity. Kai wasn't wearing a bra underneath the dress, and I have to stop myself from covering her up, hiding her small breasts from these strangers. She'd be so self-conscious. The tiny white panties she wears, I gave those to her weeks ago and couldn't wait to get back up to the room so I could peel them away. The faint marks shadowing the golden skin of her thighs and shoulders—I gave those to her too, when we made love on our wedding night.

She bruises easily, I want to tell them.

Be careful of her vocal cords, I stop myself from saying when they intubate, sliding a tube down her throat so she can breathe.

She's a singer, you know.

Do you promise to love, honor, cherish, and protect her?

Oh, God. I've already broken my vows. What kind of cruel cosmic joke is it that I've been married one day and have already failed to protect my wife? That she may die protecting me? The sirens overpower my guilty thoughts, so loud I can't focus on anything but the sight of Kai with IVs and tubes and with her dress cut open.

Once we arrive at the hospital, everything seems to go at triple speed. I don't want to let her out of my sight, but these people flood the small entryway, wheeling her away from me, their faces tight, through wide white doors. I sort through the barrage of medical jargon they hurl at each other, searching for things I understand like jagged pieces of a jigsaw puzzle. Low blood pressure. Possible collapsed lung. Bullet. Surgery.

"What's going on?" I grab the arm of one of the doctors.

Irritation crinkles his expression, and the eyes behind his glasses snap down to my hand holding him back.

"I'm sorry." I try to take a deep breath, but instead of air, I pull in panic and fear and anger. None of it helping me get the words out. "She's my wife. They haven't told me anything. I . . . please . . . just—"

"I can't tell you much until I get in there." Dr. Haddow, according to his name badge, softens his frown. "Someone will come back to tell you what's going on."

"She's pregnant." My hands plow through my hair to grip the back of my neck. "Our baby . . ."

Dr. Haddow's eyes widen. He shakes his head and turns on his heel toward the doors without responding. I follow him as far as I can. Close enough to hear him bellow.

"She's pregnant," he says, sounding almost angry. "This blood will be leaching from the baby. Where the hell is it coming from? We gotta get in there. She ready? Okay. Let's go."

And that's it. That's all. No one gives me any more information. No one tells me what's going on with my girls.

You don't know if it's a girl yet.

Kai's so much a part of me, it's like I still hear her voice answering even in my head. I hear her as clearly as the night we lay safe in our bed, and I traced the prayer wrapping around her ribs, wondering how it will look stretched over my baby growing inside her. But we're not in our bed. We're not whispering our dreams to one another like they're a secret for just us two. And we're not safe. I couldn't keep her safe.

The guilt stacks up in my chest like bricks, so heavy I have to fall to my haunches and land on my ass right there in the middle of the emergency room. Elbows to my knees, head hanging and hands pulling at my hair. People rush past, paying me no mind. No one asks me for autographs or says they love my music or wants a picture. This ER is an alternate universe where my fame and my money and any power I have are worthless currency.

"Sir." A soft voice above me interrupts my implosion. I look up into kind brown eyes set in a young, round face. They widen with recognition.

"Mister . . . Mr. Gray, I'm sorry, but we need to get some information. That was your fiancée they just brought in? Kai Pearson?"

She knows our story.

"My wife."

Her eyes get even wider.

"Excuse me?"

"She's my wife, not my fiancée."

She blinks several times, and I can almost see the images she's seen running through her mind of me down on one knee in front of Kai on a starry night, offering her a huge sapphire ring. Offering her everything and holding my breath until she accepts. She can't be more than twenty-five or six. She's not just a nurse, and this ER isn't a bubble. She probably reads US Magazine. Probably downloaded the Spotted app and gets alerts about Kai and me sent directly to her phone. Probably stalks TMZ like any other twenty-five-year-old. She blinks at me a few times before clearing her throat, setting aside the fan and asserting her professionalism.

"We'll need you to complete some basic information for us."

I'm forcing myself to my feet when Gep, Bristol, and Marlon burst through the doors, their eyes picking through the chaos until they find me.

"Rhys!" Marlon rushes over, flanked by my sister and Gep. "What's going on? Where's Kai?"

"Surgery." My voice has lost the sharpness of panic, yielding to the dullness of pain. "They won't tell me anything yet. I don't think they'll know much until they . . . until they . . ."

I close my eyes and drag my hands over my face. When I open my eyes, all three of them stare at me with the same concern.

"Kai's father is with us," Gep says. "He and his daughter are parking."

"James Pearson?" My body goes stiff, my hand freezing at the back of my neck. "He's here?"

"He called me." A frown disrupts the smooth lines of Bristol's face. "I was the one who got them their tickets and arranged for them to come backstage after the show, so he had my number."

"Here he comes." Marlon lifts his chin toward the ER entrance.

"He" is a tall man with dark hair and wide, panicked eyes. At first he looks nothing like Kai. Neither does the blonde teenaged girl at his side. But as he gets closer, I see that resemblance that has less to do with actual shared features and more to do with the unique stamp of shared DNA.

"Where is she?" he demands as a greeting, what's left of his Southern drawl swallowed up by the sharp words.

"Surgery." I try to tamp down my misplaced territorialism. He is her father, though he's been a sorry one. She's not just mine, but I hate that he is the one I have to share her with. Someone who doesn't deserve her. Who has hurt her. I don't deserve her. I've hurt her, but I love her unconditionally. And this guy's conditions abandoned Kai for fifteen years.

Before we can get any further, Dr. Haddow walks up, a frenetic energy rolling off him. He's one of those people who thrives in emergencies. Not in a bad way. In the best way. Where the rest of us get muddled and confused, everything crystallizes for them, and their responses sharpen. I thought I was one of those people until the girl I love more than my own life started turning blue in the ambulance.

"Kai Pearson's family?" His eyes dart over our little group before landing on me.

"She's my daughter," James Pearson answers immediately. "What can you tell us?"

I swallow back a sharp retort. Dr. Haddow glances my way, silently asking my permission. I nod that it's okay.

"You'll want to move to the waiting room upstairs." He hooks two fingers into the mask hanging under his chin. "We'll know more soon, but what we know now is that Kai's lung has collapsed. No exit wound. The bullet's still in there, and we think it may have clipped an artery or something vital. There's too much blood for it not to have."

I bite the inside of my jaw until it hurts. Partly to hold back a curse or a moan. I honestly don't know what would come out of me. And partly to inflict pain on myself, even though it doesn't compare to what Kai's experiencing. None of this sounds good. It sounds so much worse than anything I ever imagined Kai would have to endure because I was so careful with her. Because I would always protect her.

"We need to transfuse right away," Dr. Haddow continues. "I have to tell you, Mr. Gray, that the fetus is not our priority, but we'll do all we can to keep it viable."

All eyes land on me.

"Fetus?" James' brows drop over the questions in his eyes.

"Fetus?" Bristol echoes. "Huh?"

Dr. Haddow's eyes slide to me, an apology clearly written there.

"It's all right," I tell him before turning my attention to everyone else. "Kai's pregnant."

"Oh, my God." Bristol clenches her eyes closed and rests her fist against her lips.

Marlon slips an arm around her, and she drops her head to his shoulder. There's sympathy in his eyes when they meet mine.

"How far along is your wife?" Dr. Haddow asks.

"Wife?" The wrinkles in James' forehead disappear as his expression stretches with surprise. "How . . . you . . . you got married? When?"

"Last night." I'm losing my patience with him. He's acting like he should be here when I'm not sure he should. He's acting like he should know things about my life with Kai that I'm not sure he deserves to know. He's acting like her father, when he's been anything but for the last decade and a half.

"She's only about four weeks." I force the fear back to ask the only question that matters. "Is she still . . . is Kai . . . is the baby . . . are they gonna be okay? Are my girls gonna be okay?"

He doesn't answer quickly enough for me. I want a practiced, pat answer full of medical arrogance that she'll be fine. That they're doing all they can. That the best doctors are doing their best. He doesn't give me that.

"It's too early for me to say, Mr. Gray." He rubs at the back of his neck. "There's a lot of blood. We've inserted a chest tube to re-inflate the lung. The bullet entered through her back on the right side, and lodged in her lung. The trajectory of a bullet is unpredictable. It has a way of not staying where we think it will. We believe it may have nicked an artery. We're trying to get and keep blood out of her lungs and keep her from hemorrhaging."

He levels a careful glance my way before going on.

"The body protects what is most important for its survival." He shrugs. "It's the way we're designed. So all the blood is going where it's needed, and that is not to the fetus."

"Baby." I allow one anxious breath to say the word. "Could we just say 'baby'? 'Fetus' is . . ."

"The baby is not the priority of Kai's body right now," Dr. Haddow continues. "Survival is, and it's sending all of its resources to where it's injured. If there's any hope of saving this pregnancy, we have to transfuse right away."

"Okay." My heart lifts that he's even thinking about saving the pregnancy. "Yes. Do that. Do whatever it takes to save Kai. To save the baby."

"Kai has the most common blood type for donating, O negative," the doctor says. "Basically anyone can receive from her, but she can only receive from other O negative donors. We had a pile up last week that badly depleted our blood supply. Are any of you—"

"I'm O negative." The blonde teenager speaks up for the first time. I'd almost forgotten she was there, standing just beyond our circle. Cassie looks nothing like my girl, but there is something in her eyes—a fight, a resolve that I always assumed Kai got from circumstances. Maybe it was inherited after all.

"I had a bad cut last year." Cassie's voice gets softer with all the adults looking at her. "I found out then I was O negative."

"So am I," James says. "We'll donate. Just tell us what to do."

"Come with me right away." Dr. Haddow starts back in the direction of the double doors, not even waiting to see if James and Cassie are with him. All three of them disappear. I'm left standing there with questions and no answers. With guilt and trepidation. With barely a hope to hold on to.

But I do hold on. For my girls, I hold on.

18

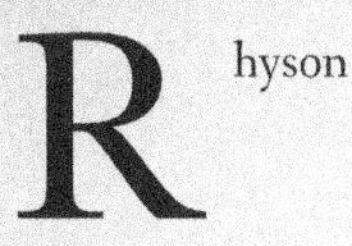

hyson

IT'S BEEN HOURS.

I think it's been hours. I'm so numb, so oblivious to everything going on around me in this damn waiting room, we could have been sitting here for a month. That's how I foresee a life without Kai. This winding meander of minutes and hours and days that blurs into an eternity. That cuts through a desert, a dry existence devoid of life that could have been rich. Could have been flooded with love, but now may be a wasteland.

"You should clean up." Bristol plops down beside me on the less-than-comfortable couch, its salmon-colored pleather cool against my back. "Ella's bringing some clothes for you."

I shrug. Why should I care how I look? How I smell? If Kai doesn't make it, I'm not sure I'll ever care about those things again.

"Ruthie is on her way." Bristol reads a text on her phone. "She just texted me from the plane we sent. They're about to take off now."

"San?"

I force myself to listen, to stay engaged because Kai loves them more than anyone else. She would want them here. I think I need them here because they are the only ones who could even come close to loving Kai as much as I do.

"Still no luck." Bristol twists her lips apologetically. "I've been ringing his cell and the hotel in Turks, but I haven't been able to reach him. I'll keep trying."

"Yeah, thanks. Keep me posted."

Bristol looks down at her phone when it rings.

"This is Ella now." She puts the phone to her ear and heads toward the exit. "Hey. Where are you?"

I think of the last time I waited in a hospital for Kai. Ella was there then too. She's a good friend. I was so anxious that night Kai collapsed, and it was just pneumonia. God, what I wouldn't give for this to be that simple. Maybe Ella will bring the same calm she carried then.

Luke and the band swung through, but we sent them back to the hotel with promises to keep them apprised. Gep sits in the corner on his laptop, probably trying to figure out how this got past us, where we went wrong. Marlon is curled up on one of the sofas asleep. He performed his ass off last night, and the demands of the showcase and all the work he's been doing for his album are catching up to him. He's had a long few days. We all have. We all look worse for wear, but I look the worst.

I glance down at my bare chest. The bloodied t-shirt is long gone, probably still in the back of that ambulance. Blood rings my knuckles, dried into the crevices, and tinges my palms. I touch my hair, finding it pulled into thick peeks stiff with the blood from my hands rolling through it. I'm disgusting, but I can't leave this spot. If there's news, if something happens, I have to be here. Not knowing is killing me. Not knowing if our baby girl is already gone. Not knowing if Kai's breathing right now. The last time I saw her, a tube was shoved down her throat. And now someone I don't know is cutting on my girl.

"Did they tell you anything when you gave blood?" I flick a look up at James Pearson seated on the couch across from me reading.

He peers at me over the round lenses of his glasses. His wife, a faded version of Cassie, came to pick up their daughter a little while ago. Cassie didn't want to leave, but she was exhausted, and there was nothing she could do to help after she and James gave blood. Which is more than I've been able to do.

"No." James shakes his head, using a finger to hold his place in the book he closes. "They took our blood and told us to wait out here."

His eyes rove over the half-naked, blood-stained mess that is me.

"Your sister's right." He takes off his glasses and holds the stem between his fingers. "You should clean up. You don't want Kai to see you like that when she wakes up."

My heart latches onto that phrase.

When she wakes up.

I clear my throat before walking over to sit beside him. I glance at the cover of the book he's reading. It's a Bible just like the reverend had at our wedding.

"You, uh, think Kai will be waking up?" I rest my elbows on my knees and glance up and back at him.

He considers me for a few moments before putting his glasses back on and opening his Bible to the spot.

"I believe she will."

My heartbeat accelerates, and it feels like this is the first time my heart has beaten in hours.

"How do you know?" I demand.

"I said I believe. I have faith."

That's not good enough. I know it sounds bad, but the faith of an adulterous pastor who abandons his family for his mistress and love child in Vegas doesn't comfort me that, if there is a God, He's on James' side.

"You don't put much stock in that, though, do you?" he asks, a smile curving his lips but not quite touching his eyes.

"No." I shake my head and blow out a defeated breath. "I don't."

"You don't put much stock in me in general, do you, son?"

"I'm not your son."

I stand up and walk over to where Bristol waits with Ella and the clothes she

brought. The young nurse who gave me paperwork to complete rounds out a little trio of eyes watching me like I might detonate any minute. They're not far off.

"For me?" I take the bag and manage a small smile for the nurse. "Are you taking me somewhere so I can freshen up?"

She nods, her brown eyes wide and shining. Please don't let her say she loves my music or she saw me in concert once or knows all my songs by heart. I don't give a shit. There's nothing like nearly losing the thing that means the most to you to show you how little everything else is actually worth. Thankfully, she's quiet as she leads me to a small bathroom down the hall.

It's the fastest shower I've ever taken. The hospital soap and shampoo smell like household cleaners, but they wash away the stench and stickiness of blood. I make quick use of them and tug on jeans, a t-shirt, and tennis shoes. I step back into the waiting room and come to a full stop.

Gep's on his feet talking with a police officer. Bristol joins them, folding her arms over her chest and double-dutching a glance between them. That look on her face that means she's just waiting for the right time to jump in.

"But we just have a few questions for Mr. Gray. I promise it won't take long." The police officer directs his words to Bristol, who I'm assuming, in her highly professional manner, just denied him. She has this very polite way of telling you things. It's not until you're out of her presence that you realize she told you to fuck yourself and you feel the sting of it. By the look on the officer's face, he's already feeling the sting.

"What's going on?"

The three of them turn to me. Gep's expression is as impassive as always. You could run over that guy's toe with a Mack truck and he wouldn't grimace. Bristol looks mad, which she often resorts to when things are out of her control. Anger is her fall back. And the officer looks like he's just doing his job.

"You needed to speak to me?" I ask him.

"I told him later would be better." Bristol flays him with a glance. "It's not the right time, officer."

"With all due respect, ma'am, we're conducting a criminal investigation," the officer says carefully. "I'm Officer Baynard, Mr. Gray. We want to figure out what happened."

"He's right, Bris." I sigh and gesture to the couch that probably still bears the imprint of my butt, I sat there so long. "What do you need to know?"

He asks basic questions about our day leading up to the event, and I answer, not sure what any of that has to do with anything.

"Had you or your fiancée met Anna Borden before tonight?" Officer Baynard asks.

"Is that her name?" I narrow my eyes and divide a sober look between the three of them. "That's who shot Kai?"

"We met her for the first time yesterday," Bristol asserts, eyes set on the hands in her lap.

"We did?" Rage climbs from the pit of my stomach over my chest and shoulders until it's a mist clouding my eyes. "When did we meet her? What are you talking about?"

"It was the girl from the meet and greet," Gep answers since Bristol seems to have lost her voice. She's biting her lip and staring at the floor. "The girl who, um . . . fell down."

The girl Kai pushed. The one she thought wanted to hurt me.

"She had a pen," I say dumbly. "It caught the light, and my . . . Kai thought it was a knife. She pushed her away from me."

In the quiet we all digest that information. Kai was right. Her instinct about the crazy girl was right. If I'd known she had this in mind, that she would hurt Kai, I would have rammed that pen in my own throat.

"Did she have anything to do with the blood on my car? The message about killing Kai?" My words barge into the awkward silence. "Was that her?"

"Mr. Gephardt did mention that incident, so we questioned her about it." Officer Baynard clears his throat and flicks a glance at Gep. "She confessed to that too, yes."

Gep and Bristol look at each other quickly and then away. They knew it was that girl and didn't tell me.

"So you're saying the girl who shot my wife," I say, my voice quaking with rage, not directed at the stupid girl, but at myself, "I gave that girl a ticket to the show."

"Actually I gave her the ticket," Bristol says softly, her eyes still fixed on the floor. "If you want to blame anyone, blame me. I'm the one who pushed for us to come."

Bristol gives voice to the silent shriek that's ripped through my head a hundred times since we climbed into that ambulance. Why did we come here? Why did I ignore my instincts? This is my fault.

"She should never have been at that show." Anger sharpens my words. "Never gotten close enough to shoot at Kai."

"Well, you were her target," the officer says unhelpfully. "She said if she couldn't have you then no one could."

It's like something out of a bad movie. It pisses me off that Kai ended up in the middle of it.

"Where is she now?" I grind the question to little bits.

"She's in custody at the station," the officer says. "Actually under suicide watch. Her plan was to shoot you and then turn the gun on herself."

"Why?" I spit out.

"Why was that her plan?" Officer Baynard's bushy eyebrows meet at the center of his forehead. "We—"

"No, why is she under suicide watch?" I slam my fist into the palm of my other hand. "Let her do it. Let her kill herself. Why are we stopping her?"

The officer doesn't know what to do with my feral response. With the anguish and rage propelling my words. I don't know what to do with them either. I need to walk away.

"Are we done?" I push the damp hair out of my eyes. "My wife is fighting for her life and for our unborn child, so excuse me if I don't want to waste another second on the loony bitch who tried to kill her."

I don't wait for his dismissal, but just walk away over to the window overlooking the street. The Vegas Strip glitters like a distant promise. Like a wavering mirage on the horizon. Is that what our happiness was? Our future? The promise of something that would never materialize?

I clench my teeth against the rage shrieking from my gut. Not at the fucking demented stalker. At myself. I did everything but pull the trigger. I gave her a ticket. Here I thought I had all my bases covered, had my girls protected from all harm, when the greatest harm was me. Was my blindness. My idiocy.

A sharp sound a few feet away distracts me from my recriminations. Bristol stands against the corridor wall, arms folded across her chest, face set into her usual obstinate lines. There's no sign of her sleek ponytail, and her hair is free and a little wild around her shoulders. Marlon stands so close I can't tell if he's caging her or protecting her, but the expression on his face is fierce, sterner than any I've seen him wear before. I can't hear what he's saying, but it must be good. It must be working. The tough line of her mouth starts to wobble when his hand cups her chin, tilts her face up. And then I see something I've only seen a few times in all the years since we were born within minutes of each other.

Bristol breaks.

Her face crumples, tears streaming over her cheeks. Marlon palms her head and presses her into his chest. She grips his elbows and shakes against him. The same guilt that's eating me alive gnaws at her. It's an intimate thing, witnessing someone fall apart, and I almost wish I hadn't seen it. Bristol's the strongest of us all. I wouldn't be able to do half of what I do without her, and to see her trembling unnerves me. Even the strongest needs someone to be weak with. I had no idea Marlon was that for Bristol.

I only knew that's what Kai is for me.

"You know," James Pearson says, startling me with his presence beside me at the window. "I may not be a preacher any more, but I can still believe. I still have faith. Do you have faith in anything, Rhyson?"

"Her," I whisper, my breath fogging the window. "Just in her."

This is not the time for fucking tears to burn my eyes, for me to have to blink to keep them from falling. I can't let them fall in front of the last man I want to see my weakness. The weak man who abandoned my girl and her mother. I bang my forehead against the glass and slam my fist into the thick pane.

"Faith!" I snap at his reflection beside mine in the window. "Ask me for something else. Ask me for money. For position. For fame. I can give you all of those things if you want them. But none of them will help her now, and you ask me for the one thing I don't have."

"You may have more than you think," he says quietly, apparently unfazed by my outburst.

"Yeah?" I turn to face him, my anger and pain for his inspection. "You want me to pray for Kai? You want me to send money to some preacher in exchange for her life? Or go to some confessional and leave a big check so things can be right? Just tell me which self-serving religious practice will save my wife and daughter, and I'll do it."

"How do you know it's a girl?"

You know those sunshowers? The weather phenomenon when it rains while the sun is shining? That's how incongruous his question seems to me. I'm using a pointless philosophical debate on religion to distract myself from how I fucked everything up inviting a madwoman to our concert, and he asks me that shit.

"What . . . huh?" I shake my head as if to clear it, when actually maybe he's the one whose head needs clearing. "What does that matter?"

"You just sound so certain." James tilts his head and squints at me like I'm one of his Bible verses vexing him. "And earlier when you were talking to Dr. Haddow you wanted him to tell you your girls were going to be okay."

"I don't see how this—"

"It's too early to tell, right?

"Too early?"

"In the pregnancy?" One side of his mouth gives in to a grin. "It's been a long time, fifteen years, but they didn't know at four weeks that Cassie was a girl. Has technology evolved that much now?"

"No, we don't . . . well, they don't know, but—"

"But you do," he says. "You know."

"Yeah. It's a girl."

"How do you know?"

"I just . . ." I shake my head again, and it has less of a clearing effect than it did even a few minutes ago. "I just know."

"No, a fact is something you know." James pats my shoulder. "Faith is, well, it's something you believe so strongly it feels like fact to you. And it's obvious to me you have a great capacity for it."

"The doctor's coming," Bristol says from across the room where she and Marlon are seated.

I tear my eyes away from James, wishing I had more time to digest what he said, but eager to hear from the doctor. Finally.

"She's out." Dr. Haddow crumples the surgical mask in his right hand and pushes the left over a face haggard with fatigue. "We got the bullet. She was really lucky because it just grazed an artery, but it was enough to cause all the blood loss."

He levels a glance at James.

"We needed a lot of blood," he says. "You and your daughter really came through for her. She could have hemorrhaged, but it never got to that point. She's in recovery now."

It's like we all breathe a collective sigh of relief. We exchange tentative smiles. I'm so grateful. It all sounds good so far, and I'm afraid to ask all the questions that burn my tongue. I'm afraid of the answers.

"So she, um, she'll be all right?" I brace for his response.

"She's not out of the woods yet," he says cautiously. "She's still on a ventilator. The chest tube is creating suction and removing air pressure from the lung cavity. That helps to keep the lung re-inflated. And there's always the risk of blood clots moving toward the heart with situations like this. Those are extremely dangerous and move fast, but we're monitoring her."

Hearing about chest tubes and blood clots scares the hell out of me, but they're monitoring her. It's under control. Now that I feel a little better about Kai, I force myself to ask the question consuming my mind.

"And our baby?" I watch Dr. Haddow's expression for any sign before he speaks. If our baby didn't make it, I'll still be immeasurably grateful that Kai did, but I won't get over it any time soon. Neither would Kai.

"As of now, still viable." A weary laugh rattles in his chest. "It's a little bit of a miracle. The odds weren't good, but the baby seems to be fine. We'll do an ultrasound to know for sure."

James and I exchange a glance at the word "miracle." I don't care if it's faith, kismet, or a stroke of luck that saved our baby. I'll take it.

I sit down on the armrest of the nearest chair. Relief weakens my knees. They're okay. Not out of the woods, but alive.

"Can I see her?"

I need to replace the last image I have of Kai. The bluish tinge to her skin. The blood running from her mouth. The tube invading her throat. Looking closer to death than life.

Dr. Haddow offers me another one of those rare smiles before responding.

"Soon."

While we wait, I realize I have missed calls from my father. Of course he's probably seen this all over the news. I've been so tuned into Kai and the baby, I've tuned out everything else.

"You talked to Dad?" I ask Bristol.

"No." She glances up from the statement about the shooting she's preparing for release. "But I talked to Mom."

Bristol and I have a little bit of a stare down. We both have complex relationships with our parents, but Bristol has a lot more tolerance for our mother than I do.

"Dad called, but I missed it."

"They were both concerned. Mom just knew you wouldn't want to talk to her." Bristol closes her laptop and devotes her full attention to me. "Is it really fair that you've forgiven Dad, but you still hold everything over Mom's head?"

"Dad didn't get me hooked on prescription drugs and refuse to send me to rehab until I got him the next check."

"Dad's no saint." Bristol compresses displeasure tightly between her lips.

"Did you get a hold of Grady?" I ask, ignoring her statement. It's never productive when we talk about our parents, and I don't have the emotional space right now to fight with my sister.

"Yeah, he and Em are coming tomorrow. They were on some couples' cruise, and it's the soonest they can get here." She re-opens the laptop. "For this statement, do you want to refer to Kai as your fiancée or your wife?"

"Wife," I reply decisively. "And just say we recently married in a private ceremony with close friends and family."

"It was a beautiful ceremony." An almost wistful smile teases Bristol's lips.

I glance down at the golden thread tied around my ring finger. I can't swallow. I press my lips against my teeth to control the emotions that overwhelm me. I almost lost her. Tonight I almost lost my whole world. I would have been like some pitiful Humpty Dumpty—irreparable and shattered. Nothing would have pieced me back together. Nothing would have ever been right in my world again. Aunt Ruthie once told me it was dangerous to love the way Kai and I do. I get that now. To be that vulnerable, to have everything hinge on another person drawing their next breath is the most helpless feeling in the world. There's a part of you that just wants to shut it down, to find a way to harden yourself. To find a way not to love at all. But I know I could never do that. Not with her. I'd rather live on the razor edge of devastation every day for the rest of my life with her than even one day without her.

Never is that more clear to me than when I finally walk into her hospital room.

I thought when I saw her, still breathing, I'd feel reassured. I'm actually scared all over again seeing the IVs, the mask over her face, the chest tube running from her back and through the little hole they've cut in her hospital gown. I don't know if it's the culmination of everything that's happened in the last few hours, or the sight of her like this, but any composure I have unravels as soon as I sit down in the chair by her bed. Kai is the one I'm weak with, and even though she's not awake, my walls can't hold with her this close.

I break down.

Like I never have before. Like someone who has been swimming upstream for hours, for days, for years, only to sink with the shore in sight. I'm drowning from the inside out. My heart thrashes inside my chest. Guilt, relief, fear. They swirl around me as I go down.

I press her small hand to my forehead and bathe her fingers in my tears as I contemplate how close I came to losing her, how close I came to a barren life without her. I'm undone. Any bravado I had, any semblance of control completely unspools at her bedside into this moaning, weeping, helpless son of a bitch who would do anything to trade places with her. Anything to take this pain away from her. That's what hurts most of all. It should be me here with a hole in my chest. Me with a collapsed lung. With a bullet hole in my back. A bullet that was meant for me.

I wouldn't even pause if I had to die for you, Rhyson.

Why did she do it? Did she think this would hurt me any less than a bullet ripping through my heart?

"I'm spanking you for this when we get outta here, Pep." I croak out a tear-soaked laugh. "And not in a sexy way."

The silence reiterates that she's not well. If I close my eyes, I can still see her at our last-minute wedding. Glowing. Healthy. Whole. Happy. I want that back so badly. I want to wind time up and hurtle it back to the night I gave in and agreed to come to Vegas. I hate this place and we're never coming back.

I reach across her prone body to find her left hand on the other side. They removed her engagement ring during surgery, but somehow that little gold thread remains tied around her finger. I search it out, stroke it like a genie's bottle, and I have one wish. That she would come back to me.

The steady beep of the machine monitoring her heart isn't what assures me she's alive. It's a different beat. The beat anchoring our melody, strong and percussive. I'm quiet and still until it thumps inside of me. Until I hear our love. That song, that refrain that hums through my very blood and inundates my soul until every note, every phrase, every measure drowns out everything else. Our song isn't one I've ever written or sung. It's the one that plays between our souls.

I look to her face, hoping our song has penetrated the dark quiet she's in, and that she'll be smiling back at me like nothing ever happened. That my love lured her from the deep sleep. Instead I see a small red line trickling from her mouth. The beep on the monitor skips and speeds, sending a warning that brings people wearing white coats and green scrubs rushing into the room with a large cart, pushing me out of the way.

"She was just fine," I yell over the commotion. "What's happening? Somebody tell me what's wrong!"

None of them seem to hear me. Everyone focuses on Kai,

hurling numbers and readings at one another over my head. I can only pick out two words that make any sense, and they pin me to the wall with icy fear.

Blood clot.

A red flat line onscreen levels me. Knocks all the breath from me like a body blow.

In the midst of chaos, I strain my ears for that beat always echoing from my heart to hers, that sound, that song I thought would connect me to her forever.

But there is no beat.

There is no sound.

There is no song.

It's gone.

19

ai

THIS FEELS LIKE HEAVEN.

I'm wrapped in cotton. Warm. Secure. Safe. The lyrics of an old hymn are written on the walls around me.

It is well with my soul.

Mama used to sing it while she made biscuits. Sometimes she would cry. I couldn't tell from pain or pleasure, but it was a beautiful sound. Mama used to say some of the best songs came from pain.

He gives us beauty for ashes, Kai Anne.

Her voice in my head is as rich and real as when she was alive, her Southern drawl slowing every word, inviting you to sit a spell.

"You brought the baby with you."

I look up, startled by the familiar voice I thought I'd never hear again and by the baby I just now realize I'm holding.

"Mama?" Shock and joy ricochet through me like a Mexican

jumping bean, so happy and frantic I almost drop the baby. My mother stands there, as beautiful as she was when I was a little girl.

"Here, let me take her." Mama cuddles the baby girl in her arms, her expression soft and awed. "She's so beautiful, Kai Anne."

I step closer to see for myself, and breathe in Mama's scent of cinnamon and pears. Her soft hair brushes against my arm. It is her. The hair hangs almost to her elbows like a long, dark night. The beautiful face I grew up with is unlined by pain, and the eyes she lifts to my face are alive and alert and beautiful. She looks nothing like the last time I saw her when she lay in her bed dying before dawn.

"Are you even looking at her?" Mama laughs and shakes her head, shifting the baby so I can see. "She looks just like you did when you were a baby."

And she does. The same dark, downy hair curling around her face. The same pink bow mouth. And those are my winged brows in flight over the slightly tilted eyes. But when she looks back at me, as sweet as baby's breath, they aren't my eyes. They're quicksilver. They're storm clouds heralding rain. She has her father's eyes.

"Where's Rhys, Mama?" I roll the panic out of my voice like lumps from dough. I knead out the fear that would rise in my chest. "Is he here? Is he with us?"

It's like Mama doesn't hear me. She's stroking the baby's chubby fingers and singing the tune that warmed our small kitchen on cold mornings.

"When peace like a river attendeth my way," she croons, looking up at me, a gentle smile curling around the words. "When sorrows like sea billows roll."

Those lyrics have always calmed my fears, eased my worries, but not now. There is only one thing that could.

"Rhyson, Mama. Where is he?" Distress spikes my voice to a higher octave. "I want him. Where is he?"

"It is well with my soul," she keeps singing.

"Rhyson." My heart is torn between staying here with Mama and this beautiful baby girl and seeking out the other half of my soul.

I don't want to leave them, but Rhyson is the distant music my ears strain to hear. If I could just get closer. I have to go. I have to—

"Pep."

A gentle shake at my shoulder startles me, jerking a sharp breath through my mouth and inflating my chest. I blink a few times until my eyes adjust to the semi-dark of the room, adjust to the time and space I've landed in. I'm not in that dream that felt like Heaven. I'm not in that hospital room, a year ago today, wrenched back to life after flat-lining. I'm in our home. In a dimly lit room with the man for whom I defied death.

A shadowy outline of broad shoulders blocks the moonlight the blinds allow through the window. There's a click and then soft light from a lamp nearby.

"I knew I was the man of your dreams," Rhyson says, a slight smile playing around his full lips. "I just didn't realize it was so literal."

"What?" I glance up at him, still orienting myself to the here and now.

"You were saying my name in your sleep." His smug smile would usually have me rolling my eyes, but that dream felt so real, even his smugness is welcome. I can't shake it off. I can't laugh it off. I just look back at him, eating up every beautiful inch of him with my eyes. I stare until his smugness slips, and concern takes its place.

"Pep, what's wrong?" He leans down to kiss my forehead. "Let me take her."

I glance down at the peaceful bundle swaddled in my arms. Our daughter Aria blinks back at me with her daddy's eyes. A wide yawn stretches her little mouth and squints her silvery eyes closed. Her lips are still shiny with milk. My silk kimono flops off my shoulder, exposing one breast. I must have fallen asleep feeding her again.

"You're probably working too hard." Rhyson leans down to take Aria, his eyes dropping to the naked nipple tipped with a drop of milk. "Aria is one lucky girl."

Rhyson chuckles when my cheeks heat up as I pull the kimono

closed over my nakedness. I had just taken a shower after an exhausting day of shooting when I heard Aria's distinct hungry cry from the nursery. Guess I was more tired than I realized. The choreography for my first video is demanding, but I love it. It's what I originally envisioned my debut video would be. I'm not sure how he got my new cell number, but Dub texted me with a simple message.

Use the tunnels.

The routine may not be what it would have been when Dub and I first brainstormed it. Who knows what we could have done as a team? I don't regret walking away from him, though. I plan to spend the rest of my life showing Rhyson he is the most important thing to me. A dance routine seems a small sacrifice.

I stand from the ancient rocking chair Aunt Ruthie brought from the attic back in Glory Falls. She said when I was a baby, it used to put me out like a light. It still does. I often fall asleep before Aria.

Rhyson is doing that subtle baby bounce, his lips to her ear. Sometimes he sings her to sleep. Sometimes he whispers to her until she gives in and drifts off. Whatever he does, he's better at getting her to sleep than anyone else. Even Aunt Ruthie.

"Is Aunt Ruthie home?" I tighten the silk knot at my waist.

"Not yet." Rhyson grins over Aria's dusky hair. "She went to a movie with one of the ladies from her yoga group."

Aunt Ruthie has definitely adapted to LA life. After the shooting, we had to be so careful with my long recovery while I was pregnant. Aunt Ruthie insisted she come stay for a while. "A while" turned into selling Glory Bee and moving in with us. It's awesome having her here, and she'll be invaluable when our little family goes on the road for my tour.

"So we're home alone, huh?" I lean up to take Rhyson's earlobe between my teeth, pressing my breast into his arm. "How long do you think it'll take you to get her to sleep?"

Our eyes collide and kindle in the nursery's dim lamplight, igniting the small space separating us. Between long hours in the studio finalizing my album, the shoot for my first video, and all

Rhyson's been doing for Prodigy, we've been missing each other. Add an infant not yet sleeping through the night, and it's been a week since we made love.

"She's almost out now." Rhyson's voice roughens with need. "Go wait for me. I'll be there soon."

I relish the fire building inside me as I walk down the hall to our bedroom. Anticipation licks across my skin and burns away the last vestiges of the dream. It's not the first time I've dreamed of Mama since Aria was born. There must be some part of me that so badly wants Aria to meet her grandma that I make it happen in my dreams sometimes.

My loyalty to Mama continues to complicate the relationship with my father. Forgiving him, trying with him, still sometimes feels like I'm betraying Mama; like I'm forgetting how he hurt her. How he hurt us. Maybe it took half his life and most of mine to make peace with his demons, but I think he has. Now he wants to make peace with me. We've spoken a few times by phone since Vegas. He flew in to see Aria when she was born, and seemed to fall in love with her instantly like any other grandpa would. Aria probably wouldn't have made it if he and Cassie hadn't been at the hospital that night. Having enough of the blood I needed so quickly to transfuse most likely saved Aria's life. It probably saved mine. That alone makes me feel better about trying, so I do.

I walk over to the large window overlooking the hills just behind our house and sigh at the hard road behind and ahead of my father and me. Things have improved some because Cassie and I talk regularly. She's a good kid, and I've encouraged her love of dance and performing as much as I have time to. I can't blame her for the actions our father and her mother took all those years ago that splintered my family.

Warm hands span my waist and pull me back into a wall of muscle. I send my fingers up over the firm line of Rhyson's neck to burrow in his hair.

"She's asleep?" I ask.

"Hopefully for the night," he says, voice husky against my neck.

His fingers deftly untie the knot sealing my kimono and he pushes my hair aside so his tongue can explore the cove behind my ear. He tugs at the shoulders of the robe until it slides down my body in a gasp of silk, hitting the floor around my ankles. I drop my head forward, and he lavishes the line of my shoulder with open-mouthed kisses. He dips to lick between my shoulder blades, and one wide palm reaches around to tug and twist my nipple.

"Rhys." My voice is an inconsequential thing under the weight of this passion. It can't hold. "That feels . . ."

His tongue wanders over to my right shoulder and he pauses over the scar interrupting the smooth plane of my back. He rests his forehead there for a few seconds, his breath growing labored behind me.

"I live you, Pep." He kisses that small spot that almost cost my life. That almost cost Aria hers.

"I live you too."

Tears collect at the corners of my eyes, and I'm so grateful to still be here with him. That night and the weeks that followed will always haunt us at least a little. How close we came to losing each other. But it only makes our days, our nights together that much richer. It only makes us that much more grateful.

His mouth is on the move again, and I feel the smallest rush of air when he squats behind me and palms my thighs. His lips whisper across the rounded cheeks of my bottom. His open mouth hot and hungry, nibbles at my curves.

"I love your ass," he whispers over the heated skin.

"Baby, please." My legs are ribbons. I can barely stand as he journeys down my legs, and suckles the vulnerable skin behind my knees. "I can't take this."

He stands, coming around to face me, twining our fingers and then walking backward to our bed, his eyes set on mine. He stops at the foot of the bed and releases my fingers. I immediately grab the hem of his t-shirt and push it over the powerful chest and shoulders until he's bare. My lips fall to his nipples where I suck and bite until his panting breath fills my ears. All the while, I grip his lean hips and persuade the sleep pants down and over his legs until he's as naked as I am.

He sits down, pulling me to straddle his thighs. Our tongues wrestle in each other's mouths. His fingers twist my hair, tugging my head back, forcing my mouth open wider for him to pillage. I'm so caught up in the desperate intimacy of this kiss, of our bodies flush and moving against each other, seeking friction, I barely notice that he's lain back and taken me with him. He pushes at my hips, sliding me up until my legs bracket his lean waist. He urges me up a few more inches until I'm spread over his chest. And a few more until I hover over his mouth.

"God, yes." His breath whistles across the part of me that needs him most. His fingers press tight into my hips when he brings me down the last few inches to his lips. The first tender licks into my pussy drive my hands to the headboard. He hums against me, opening his mouth over me to devour. We war, him holding my hips still for his feast, and me bucking into his lips and tongue, the need to move overwhelming. I release the headboard, finding my breasts heavy and bobbing with the desperate motion of my body. I twist my nipples and riot over his face, lost in the need to blow the dam holding me back.

"Ahhhh, Rhys!"

The cry rips from my throat as I come, my head tipping until my hair brushes the small of my back. He drinks of me, greedily slurping at the juices painting the insides of my thighs and running his nose up and down my divide.

I'm limp when he lifts me and lays me down. He gives me no time to recover, his lips taking my nipples, his hands stroking inside my thighs. I want to protest, to stop him because my body can't withstand another wave, but it feels too good, and before I know it, my hips are churning again, seeking him, hungry for him to fill me.

"Baby, now," I plead, opening my eyes to find him staring at me.

"You're so damn beautiful when you want me," he whispers.

"I want you all the time." I latch on to his cock, hard and ready between us, so close to where I need it to be. "I want you now."

"Wait." He presses his lips to mine. "You've gotta taste this."

His tongue forays between my lips, and my own scent crowds my senses as he feeds the sweetness to me. It's honey. It's caramel. It's crusted with confection because it's my taste on his tongue. It's the blend of him and me that soaks the lining of my mouth and slides down my throat. I moan into the kiss, spreading my legs under him as wide as I can, tempting him into my void.

"Please," I beg with jagged breath. "Now."

He nods, pushing my knees back as far as they'll go before sinking in.

"Fuck, fuck, fuck." The words fall from his lips and land against my neck as that first moment of oneness consumes us both. "I dream about this pussy. I think about it all day."

"It's yours," I gasp as our hips kiss and part, mimicking each other's motions perfectly. I hook my ankles above the muscled curve of his ass, urging him as deep as he can go. He slams into me, knocking the air from my chest. I arch up, my neck curving an invitation for his lips. He sucks the skin, deliberately marking me as his. He rocks into me harder than he ever has, deeper than he ever has. I grip him more tightly than I ever have, scoring his back, trying to claw through skin and drill through bone until I reach soul.

The headboard knocks a sex-charged rhythm against the wall. Rhyson presses up to capture my eyes with his, the muscles of his arms strained, his hands fisted on the pillow beside my head as he plunders me. I could get lost in these eyes that possess me from above. I could get lost in this room, in this love that swallows up every fear and every doubt, and leaves me absolutely certain my life is here. My life is his. And as he comes inside me strangling a groan in his throat and slamming a fist into the tufted headboard, I know his life is mine.

Like a conductor with a baton, he brings us down in concert. His hips slowing our rhythm to nothing. His breath easing in my ear until my shallow breaths match his deeper ones. His palm rolls up and down my leg still wrapped around and holding him close. By inches, he rolls us until we face one another in the bed, our bodies still unified.

"We can't go a week again." He pushes the tousled mass of my hair out of my eyes. "We might seriously injure each other one day fucking like that."

Laughter bubbles up in me and spills onto the pillow we share.

"You went six weeks after Aria was born." I lovingly trace the bold lines of his nose and chin and cheekbone.

"'Self-improvement is masturbation,'" he quotes, brows upping and downing suggestively.

"I cannot believe you're quoting Fight Club when my brain still isn't working properly."

"Your brain's working well enough to recognize the quote." He slowly slides out of me, a reluctant separation of our bodies. He props up on his elbow and starts lifting my hair and letting it fall.

"I love your hair long like this." A grin softens the beautiful austerity of his face. "But I'd probably love it buzzed as long as it's attached to you."

I haven't cut my hair since Aria was born, and it hangs almost to my elbows. The weight stretches most of the wave out, and it pours down my back nearly bone straight, longer than I've worn it since I was a child. I look in the mirror each morning surprised by how much more it makes me look like Mama.

"I had that dream again," I confess quietly. He stiffens beside me, the hair falling from his fingers unnoticed as his eyes zero in on mine. "The one where Aria and I are in Heaven with my mom and I can't find you."

He doesn't say anything, but cradles my cheeks between his warm palms and kisses me. It's tinged with desperation and gratitude. He hates that dream. It's bittersweet for me because I see my mother exactly as I want to remember her, but it's always filmed with fear until I wake up and find Rhyson beside me. I return the kiss in full measure. One day my heart may burst from this love that burgeons, that overflows. Not a day goes by that I don't thank God for sparing my life. For sparing Aria's. Really for sparing Rhyson's because I know he would have been a shell of himself if he'd lost us.

"I want to dedicate Aria," I whisper into our kiss. He goes still and pulls back, peering at my face in the light of our bedside lamp.

"Is that like sprinkling her or something?" His eyes narrow suspiciously.

Poor Aria. The only person Rhyson's more protective of than me is that baby. He knows where she is every minute of every day. He went a little overboard for a while after Vegas. We barely left the house. He was obsessed with no one ever getting a photo of me once I started showing. He doubled the security team, even though Gep assured him it was unnecessary. I didn't give him a hard time about it because he told me how it felt to hold me bleeding in his arms. How helpless he felt standing against the wall while I flat-lined.

It still haunts me too. As much as I look forward to this tour, there's a part of me dreading it. I haven't been onstage in front of a live audience since the shooting. I have no idea how I'll respond, but I've admitted to myself and to Rhyson that I'm anxious. So is he. I'm the one who was shot, but sometimes I think Rhyson bears the deepest scars.

He turns me over to cradle my bottom against him, and my back presses into his chest.

"Not sprinkling, no," I answer once we're settled.

"So what does it mean to be dedicated? It sounds like a pagan ritual."

"It's not." I laugh until I feel the vibration of him laughing back. "The Baptists don't do pagan. Believe me."

"You were dedicated?"

"Yeah. My father actually dedicated me himself." I force back sudden emotion before going on. "It signifies that parents trust God to take care of their child. That ultimately it's His child, and they have faith He'll take care of His own."

Rhyson's silent behind me so long that I twist my neck to see him.

"Faith, huh?" He nods, a small smile curving his mouth. "Where do we do it?"

"We could do it at Aunt Ruthie's new church." I grin up at him. "Leave it to Aunt Ruthie to find a Southern Baptist church in LA. She says no grandbaby of hers is growing up a heathen."

Rhyson's fingers stroke over my stomach until they reach the prayer wrapped around my ribs.

Now I lay me down to sleep. I pray the Lord my soul to keep. If I should die before I wake, I pray the Lord my soul to take.

"Are you gonna teach Aria that prayer?" Rhyson's fingers are gentle over the tattoo.

So many things from my childhood still shape me, especially the simplicity of my family's faith. A faith sorely tested and sometimes even broken. But those nights Mama knelt by the bed and whispered that prayer with me, those nights I'll carry with me forever.

"Yeah. I think I will."

I huddle into the man who has stolen my heart and healed my soul, closing my eyes with peace as my lullaby.

When peace like a river attendeth my way.

I'm wrapped in cotton. Warm. Secure. Safe.

This feels like Heaven.

Also by Kennedy Ryan

Now that you've finished Rhyson + Kai's story, don't you want to know what happens with Grip + Bristol?

Find out in THE GRIP TRILOGY

(Available in Kindle Unlimited)

Grip Box Set - All 3 Books in 1

In Kindle Unlimited

(includes exclusive BONUS material)

Or

Individual Grip Trilogy Titles

In Kindle Unlimited

Flow (Grip 1)

https://geni.us/FlowAmazon

Grip (Grip 2)

https://geni.us/GripAmazon

Still (Grip 3)

https://geni.us/StillAmazon

THE HOOPS SERIES - All in Kindle Unlimited

(3 Interconnected Standalone Stories)

Ebook, Audio & Paperback

LONG SHOT (A HOOPS Novel)

Iris & August's Story

https://geni.us/LSAmazon

BLOCK SHOT (A HOOPS Novel)

Banner & Jared's Story

https://geni.us/ReelOnAudible

HOOK SHOT (A HOOPS Novel)

Lotis & Kenan's Story

https://geni.us/HShotAmazon

HOOPS Box Set (All 3 in 1)

https://geni.us/HoopsBoxSet

HOOPS Shorts (A HOOPS Novella Collection)

https://geni.us/HOOPSShortsAll

* * *

ALL THE KING'S MEN

Ebook, Audio & Paperback

The Kingmaker (Duet Book 1 - Lennix & Maxim)

https://www.bloombooks.com/the-kingmaker.html

The Rebel King (Duet Book 2 - Lennix & Maxim) Kindle Unlimited

Ebook, Audio & Paperback

https://www.bloombooks.com/the-rebel-king.html

Queen Move (Kimba & Ezra)

https://geni.us/QueenMovePlatforms

Skyland Series

Before I Let Go (Standalone Book 1)

https://geni.us/BeforeILetGo

*****Reel (Standalone Book 1)*****

The Hollywood Renaissance Series

AVAILABLE NOW in Kindle Unlimited!

Buy: https://geni.us/Reel

A Hollywood tale of wild ambition, artistic obsession, and unrelenting love.

Directors. Actors. Producers. Costume Designers. Musicians. Writers.

A world where creatives make art and make love!

The Close-Up,

A Hollywood Renaissance/HOOPS Novella

mybook.to/TheCloseUp

THE BENNETT SERIES

When You Are Mine (Bennett 1)

Loving You Always (Bennett 2)

Be Mine Forever (Bennett 3)

Until I'm Yours (Bennett 4)

Connect With Kennedy!

Connect With Kennedy!

kennedyryanwrites.com

On Facebook, join my reader group for updates, fun and insider scoop:

Reader Group:
bit.ly/KennedyFBGroup

Never miss sales, new releases, and get a free book every month when you join my Mailing List: subscribepage.com/kennedyryan

New Release Text Alerts:
Text KennedyRyan to (678) 647-7912

TikTok: @kennedyryanauthor.

Like On Facebook

Instagram: kennedyryan1

Twitter: @kennedyrwrites

Bookbub

Follow on Amazon

Follow on Book + Main

* * *

A RITA® and Audie® Award winner, *USA Today* bestselling author **Kennedy Ryan** writes for women from all walks of life, empowering them and placing them firmly at the center of each story and in charge of their own destinies. Her heroes respect, cherish, and lose their minds for the women who capture their hearts. Kennedy and her writings have been featured in Chicken Soup for the Soul, *USA Today, Entertainment Weekly, Glamour, Cosmopolitan, TIME, O* magazine, and many others. She is a wife to her lifetime lover and mother to an extraordinary son.

Made in United States
North Haven, CT
04 April 2024